Praise for the Inspector DeKok Series by Baantjer

"Along with such peers as Ed McBain and Georges Simenon, [Baantjer] has created a long-running and uniformly engaging police series. They are smart, suspenseful, and better-crafted than most in the field."
—*Mystery Scene*

"Baantjer's laconic, rapid-fire storytelling has spun out a surprisingly complex web of mysteries."
—*Kirkus Reviews*

"DeKok is a careful, compassionate policeman in the tradition of Maigret; crime fans will enjoy this book."
—*Library Journal*

"DeKok's maverick personality certainly makes him a compassionate judge of other outsiders and an astute analyst of antisocial behavior."
—*The New York Times Book Review*

"It's easy to understand the appeal of Amsterdam police detective DeKok; he hides his intelligence behind a phlegmatic demeanor, like an old dog that lazes by the fireplace and only shows his teeth when the house is threatened."
—*The Los Angeles Times*

"A major new voice in crime fiction for America."
—*Clues: A Journal of Detection*

"Baantjer seduces mystery lovers. Inspector DeKok is part Columbo, part Clouseau, part genius, and part imp."
—*West Coast Review of Books*

"... supports the mystery writer's reputation in his native Holland as a Dutch Conan Doyle. His knowledge of esoterica rivals that of Holmes, but Baantjer wisely uses such trivia infrequently, his main interests clearly being detective work, characterization, and moral complexity."
—*Publishers Weekly*

"There's no better way to spend a hot or a cold day than with this man who radiates pleasure, adventure, and overall enjoyment. A five-star rating for this author ..."
—*Clues: A Journal of Detection*

"DeKok's American audiences can delight in his work. Descriptive passages decorate the narrative like glittering red Christmas baubles."
—*Rapport*

Other Inspector DeKok Mysteries

DeKok and Murder by Melody
DeKok and the Geese of Death
Murder in Amsterdam

DeKok and
THE DEATH OF A CLOWN

by
A. C. BAANTJER

Translated by H. G. Smittenaar

speck press
denver

Library of Congress Cataloging-in-Publication Data

Baantjer, A. C.
[De Cock en de dood van een clown. English]
Dekok and the death of a clown / by A.C. Baantjer ; translated by H.G.
Smittenaar.
p. cm.
ISBN-13: 978-1-933108-03-2
ISBN-10: 1-933108-03-7
I. Smittenaar, H. G. II. Title.

PT5881.12.A2D56613 2005
839.3'1364--dc22

2005029688

1

"I'm not a swindler."

Inspector DeKok of the renowned police station at Amsterdam's Warmoes Street gazed at the man in front of him with a searching look.

"Why do you say that?" he asked sharply. "I haven't accused you of anything, least of all swindling."

The man nervously played with the buttons of his pearl-gray waistcoat. The inspector's cool observation made him restless.

"I ... eh, I expect you'll have a lot of questions once I tell you my story."

DeKok nodded calmly.

"That's my job," he said soothingly. "But you would have no chance to be heard, should I assume you came to the police just to tell a fraudulent story."

The man gave DeKok a grateful look.

"The thing is, my situation is somewhat ridiculous. It stretches even my imagination. That's what makes me so insecure. It is as though I blacked out for a time."

DeKok's eyebrows rippled briefly. The man did not notice.

"Have you had an accident? Have you been unconscious?"

The man shrugged.

"A few years ago I hurt my head in a car accident. But I've long since healed. My recollection of the incident is vague. There weren't any noticeable aftereffects." He shook his head. "This is something else entirely ... an inexplicable gap in *time*." He took off his glasses and polished them with his necktie. Then he rubbed the corners of his eyes with his thumb and forefinger. "During this lost time my life spun out of control."

DeKok leaned forward. His elbows rested on the desk. There was an expression of friendly understanding on his face. He could muster considerable patience.

"Let's recapitulate," he said, as if it were a treat. "You are Julius Vlaanderen, fifty-five years old, and a real estate broker. Well off?"

"Reasonably."

DeKok smiled.

"Not to worry. I don't work for the Inland Revenue."

The broker hesitated only a moment.

"I own the building along Gentleman's Canal. I have a retreat, a small chalet in Switzerland, and a few other properties. There is also a valuable collection of antique jewelry. Collecting is my hobby." It sounded apologetic.

"And part of your jewelry collection is missing?"

"Exactly."

"You estimate the missing pieces have a value of about one million?"

"It would come to about a million Euros, yes."

"Gone from your safe?"

"Yes."

"There isn't the slightest sign of a break-in?"

"That's right."

DeKok continued steadily.

"You say you're the only one with a key to the safe and the only person who knows the combination?"

Mr. Vlaanderen sighed deeply.

"My attorney keeps a spare key. He also has a sealed envelope with the combination inside. You understand ... in case anything happens to me. Although I felt it was unnecessary, upon the insistence of my son, Maurice, I asked my lawyer if everything was still intact."

"And?"

"He assured me everything in his office was undisturbed—the envelope and the key are in his safe. They have not been moved, or touched."

"What's the name of your lawyer?"

"Waarden."

DeKok pulled out his lower lip and let it plop back. It was a vulgar gesture and made an unpleasant sound. It was one of DeKok's least endearing habits. He was blissfully unaware.

"So you are completely at a loss to explain the disappearance of the jewelry from your safe?"

The broker was dispirited.

"I can think of no plausible possible scenario," he said. "This particular collection of jewelry was only in my house a few days. I recently acquired the pieces. I was delighted to get them. Last Saturday I made a formal inventory. My son was present, to assist with the inventory process. Once we finished I placed the collection in the safe. Afterward I recall closing and locking the safe, as usual. Since Saturday the key has not been out of my possession. Besides," he added, "the key is useless without the combination."

DeKok remained silent. Without embarrassment he studied the broker closely. He scrutinized, but with a professional eye. No one could have read his expression, but no detail escaped him. The inspector's non-committal stare usually made the guilty squirm with discomfort. But Vlaanderen was composed, having told his story twice.

DeKok looked at a handsome man, considering his age. His face was symmetrical, sharply delineated, accentuated by a sharp chin. His dark-blond hair was lightly gray at the temples. The coat and waistcoat reminded DeKok of Dr. Koning, the coroner. Both men appeared to have stepped out of a period film. In Vlaanderen's case it was not the outfit. His suit was formal, but a modern cut. Perhaps it was the way he carries himself, thought DeKok. Vlaanderen also lacked the absent-minded, dreamy look in the eyes of the coroner. His steel-blue eyes were sharp and alert.

"The jewels were already insured?"

The broker waved a hand with an irritated gesture.

"Of course I had them insured as the ink dried on the bill of sale. But what do you think the insurance company will say when I approach them with my story?"

DeKok smiled.

"Question marks?"

Vlaanderen nodded emphatically.

"Exactly. The story sounds like a clumsy attempt at fraud. In any event, the contract excuses the company from paying any unsubstantiated claim of theft. I'll have to double check that with my attorney." He shook his head. There was a sad look on his face. "I don't expect financial relief. My only chance is the hope you will be able to find the jewelry and/or the thief. All I can offer is my inventory, with a detailed description of each piece. Most are unique and easily recognizable."

DeKok pulled the list in front of him and silently read it. The descriptions were indeed very detailed, reflecting

Vlaanderen's love, interest, and appreciation of the pieces. It also showed that Vlaanderen was more than a knowledgeable collector. He was a true connoisseur of period jewelry. Some of the descriptions approached the lyrical.

"How long have you been collecting antique jewelry?"

"I started very young, as long as I can remember."

DeKok tapped the list.

"Do you have photos or drawings of the newest additions?"

"I can get those for you."

DeKok put the list aside.

"Does Maurice live with you?"

"Yes, until the end of this year. He's soon to marry."

"Any other people live in the house?"

Vlaanderen shook his head.

"I have a few servants, but none who live in and none who work weekends."

DeKok held his head to one side.

"What about ... eh, ... your wife?"

Vlaanderen spread his hands.

"We divorced more than eight years ago. My wife had an affair. She and her young friend now live in Paris." He gave DeKok a tired smile. "Since the affair, which caused me a lot of sorrow, I have avoided steady entanglements."

"Have you a girlfriend?"

"I date casually."

"And last weekend?"

The broker hesitated. He waited long seconds before he finally spoke.

"Indeed," he said hesitantly. "My companion arrived Saturday evening, before dinner. She left early Sunday morning."

"And on Monday morning you discovered the theft?"

"Yes."

DeKok leaned back in his chair. His brain was working overtime, trying to discern some truth regarding the strange disappearance. Suddenly he leaned forward. "Mr. Vlaanderen, do you talk in your sleep?"

After the broker left, DeKok handed the list of vanishing jewelry to his assistant, friend, and partner, Detective Dick Vledder. The two were virtually inseparable and made an excellent team. Vledder's youth, stamina, enthusiasm, and administrative strengths complemented DeKok's experience and unshakeable steadiness. Both possessed intimate knowledge of Amsterdam, in the case of the senior inspector, the seamier sides of the Dutch capitol. Vledder's ability to turn out flawless reports offset his partner's reluctance to bog either down in the paper chase. DeKok counted on Vledder's discretion, often saying, "Please put this on the telex and make sure the descriptions are included. Just say that the pictures will come later." Vledder often saved them both from his partner's vocal contempt for the police bureaucracy.

The brilliant, outspoken Inspector DeKok was decidedly eccentric. He had reluctantly entered the twentieth century, never mind the twenty-first. He still spoke of the "telex," although it had long since been replaced by faxes and computers. He still regretted the loss of handheld telephones with operators to make the connections. He would never, he often said, get used to push-button phones and automatic dialing. Self-sufficient by nature he deplored lack of personal touch and accountability. He trenchantly refused to speak with any answering machine.

Vledder hesitated and stared at the list.

"You want to pursue this little drama?" he asked, disbelief in his tone of voice.

DeKok looked surprised.

"Why wouldn't we?"

"Well," said Vledder, "we're Homicide."

"What does that have to do with anything? The man came to see us, so it's our case."

"But shouldn't we turn it over to one of the other guys?"

"Why should we? We don't have a homicide to investigate and we're police officers. A possible crime has been reported by a responsible citizen and we'll investigate."

Vledder grinned.

"There's no crime! So the jewelry supposedly vanished. How does a thief steal jewelry from a safe nobody can crack?"

DeKok rubbed the bridge of his nose with his pinky finger.

"Who says," he continued in a low tone, "nobody got the safe open?"

Vledder sank down in his chair and raised his hands over his head. Then he lowered them with a gesture of exasperation.

"But you heard what Vlaanderen said. He's the only one with a key and he's the only one who knows the combination." He paused for a moment before he continued. "The only possibility is he robbed himself," he concluded.

"Why?"

"He wanted the insurance money."

DeKok shook his head.

"If Vlaanderen set out to defraud the insurance company," he explained patiently, "he could certainly rig a burglary ... complete with clear evidence of a break-in. He could have done it in such a way it would look like an outside job. For a time, at least, he could probably bring us along with manufactured evidence. Then he'd have an outside chance of swindling the insurance company. Let's face it. He knows his absurd story will never wash with the dullest cop or insurance investigator. Don't forget, most insurance adjustors are ex-cops, or have equivalent training."

DeKok looked at Vledder while he rummaged in a drawer. He found a peppermint and popped it in his mouth.

"And I agree with Vlaanderen," he continued. "If he brings this story to the insurance company, no way will the company pay the claim. Except for a long-established relationship, why would they take his word at face value? Regardless of the presence or absence of a liability clause, he's got nothing."

"But you do?"

"What?"

"You do take his word unequivocally?"

DeKok nodded slowly.

"I see no reason to doubt his word, no matter how far-fetched his story. The mere fact Julius Vlaanderen had the courage to approach us with such a sketchy story speaks to his trustworthiness."

Vledder shook his head thoughtfully.

"Every day," he said, "the police are inundated by people with idiotic stories."

"Vlaanderen is not an idiot ... not a sensation seeker. He is not the type who seeks out notoriety. On the contrary, I think he's an intelligent, good man."

Vledder grinned his disbelief.

"Come on. He's not all that good," Vledder smirked. "He dates *casually*? He later admitted to engaging his Saturday night companion from some escort service. He recalled only her first name, Clarisse, and the considerable sum he paid for her services."

DeKok did not react. He did not feel like pursuing a fruitless discussion about the broker's ethics. Regardless of anything else, the broker's carefully prepared inventory convinced him the jewelry existed. He reasoned the collection had to be somewhere.

The question was, where?

DeKok knew they'd entered a race against time. Professionals on both sides of the law know antique jewelry falling into the wrong hands is soon disassembled, piece by piece. Experts deftly lift the stones from their unique settings. Next they melt the settings down. The stones and metal may leave the country. Certain distinctive stones and cuts can be traced, but not without difficulty. Their intrinsic value, even in an altered condition, makes the enterprise highly profitable.

He had not told the broker of that possibility because he felt the mere thought would be unbearable to an avid collector. To him the jewelry was irreplaceable.

DeKok looked at Vledder who continued to stare at the list.

"We have to try and identify the companion, Clarisse. Perhaps you can contact the Vice Squad and see if they have anything on her?"

Vledder nodded and DeKok watched him make a note of it. There was no Vice Squad in the station house. DeKok reflected on that anomaly. Warmoes Street Station was on the edge of the Red Light District. The district encompassed the old inner city of Amsterdam. It was a virtual labyrinth of narrow streets, small canals, quaint bridges, dark, narrow alleys, unexpected squares, and architectural wonders. This centuries-old neighborhood wakened to its business day at dusk. The streets offered an array of eating and drinking establishments. Exotic, often beautiful women and well-heeled pimps abounded. Endless streams of the sex-starved and the obsessed found their way to this hub. Locals mixed with busloads of international tourists. It was a nightly carnival, unlike any in the world. Vice certainly existed elsewhere in the world. The crucial difference was the remarkable tolerance of the Dutch. The district indulged her patrons in exchange for a hefty return on investment. Gratification was a commodity, not an occasion for raised eyebrows. It was clean on the surface because savvy investors kept up appearances.

Location made the old police station at Warmoes Street the busiest police station in Northern Europe. The hundreds of thousands of visitors to the district created both problems, and opportunities. Crimes ranged from petty and opportunistic to calculated and brutal. Bar patrons complained of watered or spiked drinks. Barkeeps complained of being stiffed. Bar fights erupted in their establishments. Pickpockets (many of them prostitutes) and muggers stalked the unwary. Then there was the occasional murder. But the station did not have a Vice Squad.

"I also think," continued DeKok, "we should have a little talk with Maurice, the son."

Vledder looked up from his notes.

"So, you're determined to pursue the case?"

DeKok merely nodded and pointed at the list.

"I would hurry with the telex. Every minute counts."

Vledder sighed his acceptance.

"All right," he said, "but it's an odd job for homicide detectives."

DeKok ignored the remark. Vledder was just as aware as he

was that there was no real Homicide Squad in the Amsterdam Municipal Police. The homicide detail for the entire city of Amsterdam was smaller than that in a single New York police station. Homicide detectives were spread out. He and Vledder *were* Homicide at Warmoes Street. Additional one- and two-person teams were spread out over half the remaining station houses in the city, and there was a relatively large detail at headquarters to assist individual teams. The rest, such as crime scene investigators, the crime lab, and the various pathological services had to be shared by all the different branches, such as Narcotics and, even, the Traffic Police.

Fortunately there were few murders in Amsterdam, so it was natural the small homicide teams would do other police work. Vledder had been spoiled, if you could call it that thought DeKok, by a recent string of homicide cases in their jurisdiction. There had been about twenty cases in a relatively short period of time. True, some of the cases had involved multiple victims, but it was still a small number for such a large city, particularly considering its augmented population of more than ten million visitors per year.

Vledder had just saved his completed report to disk when the phone rang. He picked it up. DeKok watched his face as the young man spoke. Vledder paled. After a while he replaced the receiver.

"Well, you can forget about vanishing jewelry," said Vledder.

"How is that?" asked DeKok, suspecting the answer.

"We have a dead clown."

"A clown? As in a circus clown?"

"Yes," answered Vledder, getting out of his chair.

"Where?" asked DeKok, following his example.

"At the bottom of Criers' Tower."

2

They waved goodbye to the watch commander as they exited the station. Outside Vledder hustled toward the car, but DeKok stopped him.

"We'll get there more quickly on foot," said DeKok. "It's only three alleys away."

"Which alleys?"

DeKok gave him a disapproving look.

"Old Side's Arm, Peaceful Citizen, and Watergate. It's about time," he chided, "you get more familiar with the immediate area around the station house. Racing around in cars, no wonder you don't know the shortcuts."

Vledder growled.

"I can never keep all those crazy alleys apart. Some won't even take two bicycles side by side."

He quickly stepped ahead. The gray sleuth followed at a more measured pace in his trademark shuffling gait. It never entered his mind to hurry. In no time at all, his young colleague was fifty feet away. At the entrance of Old Side's Arm Alley, he waited and beckoned impatiently for DeKok to catch up.

When DeKok reached him, the old man grinned.

"A dead clown is a dead clown," he said calmly. "A police relay team cannot change that."

Vledder snorted his disapproval.

"But you can't just amble along on your way to a murder."

DeKok ambled on, undisturbed.

Vledder finally adjusted his pace to that of his partner. As usual it was busy in the quarter. A constant stream of prospective customers filed past the windows with soft red and pink lights that highlighted scantily clad women. On certain corners young heroin whores offered their services. Depending on the trade, they were dull-eyed and passive or aggressively bold. The old inspector knew many by name and nickname. He knew their past and present lives. Sadly he could foresee the future. These unfortunate women competed with prostitutes who chose "the life," selling their bodies to feed addiction. Their abbreviated careers often ended in death by overdose. Many of his colleagues termed these deaths accidental, but DeKok was not so sure. He suspected many simply saw no way out, and opted for the last, lethal, fix.

It was getting darker and swirls of fog clung to the damp walls of the canals. Soon the canals would refresh themselves. Fresh water from Ijssel Lake would pump into the canal system, flushing the brackish water out to the North Sea.

DeKok stretched as he turned the last corner. To the left of The Criers' Tower was a police car, blue lights rotating on the roof. Several uniformed constables stood to the right, in front of the iron fence. One came forward and saluted the two inspectors with a hand to his cap.

"I have called for the water police and a boat. There's no other way to reach the victim."

"Why is that?"

The constable gestured.

"The dead guy is at the bottom of the tower, on a

wooden pier, just above the water surface. There are stairs, but the entrance is closed with an iron gate."

"How do you know it's a man?"

"I climbed the fence." He gave DeKok a measuring look. "I wouldn't advise you to try it. It's a bit of a climb."

"How did he die?"

The constable grimaced.

"He has a large knife sticking out of his back."

"And you're certain he's dead?"

The constable nodded.

"Yes, sir. He's gone cold."

DeKok seemed surprised.

"Cold?" he repeated.

"I felt for a pulse. Without touching or moving anything, I had to know whether we had a shot at a rescue."

DeKok nodded his understanding.

"You were right. First Aid is the priority." He looked around. "Who discovered the corpse?"

The young constable hesitated for a moment.

"We ... eh, we were patrolling along Prince Henry's Quay when a man waved at us from the edge of the sidewalk." He looked at his watch. "That was about fifteen minutes ago. We stopped. The man pointed in this direction and said there was dead clown at the bottom of Criers' Tower. Initially we thought it was some kind of joke ... he'd obviously been drinking. Just to be on the safe side, we took a look."

"Do you have the name of that man?"

"No, as I said, we thought he was playing a prank."

DeKok walked along the iron fence. The sharp odor of urine overwhelmed his sense of smell. The walls of the old tower had been used as a water closet for centuries.

The Criers' Tower, literally, "Tower of Tears," was built in

1487. It was here women gathered to send their men off to sea for years. Many would never return. The open water of the Zuyder Zee was much closer to the tower in those times. Today bronze plaques commemorate the role of this passage in history. One plaque remembers Henry Hudson, who sailed past the tower aboard his *Half Moon* in 1609 en route to the New World. The Hudson River bears his name. His expedition was sponsored by the Dutch government, who were looking for a northern route to the East Indies.

As DeKok grew numb to the reek of urine, he looked up. The top of the fence was rather high, at least nine feet. At the top, the metal bars ended in sharp points against a darkening sky.

He looked down through the bars. He could barely discern the wooden platform. It was almost completely covered by a glistening white clown costume. A bit above the waist a large knife was buried into the body, surrounded by a pool of dark blood.

DeKok stood there and stared.

The scene fascinated him, the setting surreal. This murderer, he bitterly thought, had a sinister appreciation of the grotesque. A combination of instinct and experience told the inspector he was taking on an unpredictable adversary. This was someone whose psyche demanded more than mere revenge or the gratification of passion. This was an individual for whom dramatic impact was paramount.

Vledder came to stand next to him and they stared at the corpse together.

"That's Pierrot," said Vledder.

"But such costumes are not uncommon—maybe, even, available to rent?" DeKok sounded hesitant.

The young inspector looked serious.

"No. I mean he *is* Pierrot," he clarified with emphasis. "It isn't just the suit. I'm almost certain he performed in the Variety Revue last year. He is unique in Holland, he fashioned his persona after the original."

"Pierrot."

Vledder nodded.

"I don't know his real name, but that's his stage name."

DeKok waved in the direction of the police cruiser.

"Why don't you get on the radio and have headquarters check with the theater. We'll have his name in a few minutes. Otherwise they can probably locate his manager."

Vledder walked away. DeKok was above using the radio himself. He was inflexible regarding modern gadgets, but only too willing to have others use them to achieve results. When it came to technology, DeKok reminded Vledder of a starving vegetarian, confronted with having only ham to eat. The vegetarian would point at the ham and call it salmon. DeKok had the same ability to use technology without acknowledging it as such.

Meanwhile DeKok took a few steps back. He soaked up every detail of the surroundings. It was his special gift. Nothing escaped him. This combined with a nearly photographic memory contributed to a remarkable degree of effectiveness.

Just past the iron fence there was a kind of addition to the tower. This section was sealed by a heavy door protected by a second door fashioned of cast-iron bars. To the right of the door was mounted a small, square, white enamel plate with the number "94" painted on it in black letters.

DeKok walked back to the fence and studied the lock on the gate. It was old, simple in construction, and very rusty—it certainly had not been used in years. He considered for a moment, but decided it was senseless to try and open the lock. He took hold of one of the bars with both hands and pulled hard. There was no give. The gate did not move an inch.

DeKok reasoned the corpse had not reached the landing stage by way of the street. If the young constable, indeed, found the body cold, death likely occurred elsewhere. The voluminous white costume was visible from any vantage point. Some passerby would have seen it long before cooling occurred. DeKok had learned early in his career it took hours for a corpse to become cold, even in very low temperatures. He objectively speculated about the progress of rigor mortis.

He needed another look at his victim, whose face was hidden. The man's chin rested on the wooden deck. A bit of ruffled collar was visible. A patch of bright red hair stuck out of a white silken cap or hood.

Suddenly DeKok felt the urge to climb the fence, despite his age and 200 pounds. This viewing from a distance irritated him. It left too many questions.

Vledder returned from the cruiser. He held a notebook in his hand. With a nonchalant gesture he pointed toward the corpse.

"Pierrot's real name is Pieter Eikelbos."

"They knew at the theater?"

Vledder nodded.

"Oh, yes, he's been an artist for more than twenty-five years."

"He had always been a clown?"

Vledder shrugged.

"I didn't ask that. According to the guy at headquarters, the people at the theater were so shocked he didn't get much." He paused. "I also asked about the Water Police boat."

"And?"

"It's on the way, should be here any minute."

Bram Weelen, the police photographer, tapped DeKok on the shoulder. With a stubby index finger he pointed at his watch.

"What's up, DeKok? This must be the second time you've got me out at a reasonable time of day. Are you changing your lifestyle? No more ungodly hours?" He grinned. "Before long I'll have a regular nine-to-five job, if you're not careful." He looked around. "Where's the victim?"

DeKok smiled.

"You'll have to meditate on patience. There's no way to reach it from here with all your paraphernalia ... unless you want to climb the fence."

Bram looked at the fence with a disapproving look.

"No thanks. I'm determined to reach a respectable age and collect my pension." He approached the fence and looked down. With a startled look he turned around.

"Why, it's a ... a clown."

"Pierrot, a. k. a. Pieter Eikelbos," was the answer.

The photographer again looked at the small dock.

"Don't you guys have a boat?"

DeKok pointed to a low, gray launch that slowly turned alongside the quay. The Water Police had arrived.

"Your wish is my command," joked DeKok. Then he waved around. "If I were you I'd take a few long shots first, as long as there's just the corpse down there. Before long the place will be crawling. I'd prefer good pictures of the situation as it is now. I want a record of the position of the corpse from here and from the quay."

Weelen placed his aluminum suitcase on the street and took out his revered Hasselblad. As he fussed adjusting the lights, he looked up.

"What's this about wishes being commands?"

DeKok laughed. From the corner of his eye he saw the coroner arrive. The old man, Dr. Koning, was, as usual, dressed in an old fashioned tailcoat with striped trousers. He was followed by two morgue attendants with a stretcher. They towered over the old coroner like two Paladins of Death.

DeKok's face lit up. He walked toward the old man and shook his hand. Somehow the gray spats and the old, greenish Garibaldi hat went well with the doctor's outfit. Dr. Koning was a comforting sight.

DeKok pointed at the launch.

"We'll get you aboard. Sorry, there is no other way to reach the corpse."

"Is it a drowning?"

DeKok shook his head.

"The victim is on a small, wooden dock, just above the water line. He has a very large knife in his back."

A hefty constable lifted the slight coroner onto the launch. The elderly man crept cautiously along the narrow gangway toward the small foredeck of the launch. DeKok followed. As the launch nudged the dock they remained standing for a while, looking at the corpse. After a few seconds Koning gave the inspector a sober look.

"I hope," said the coroner seriously, "that you'll be able to find the murderer quickly."

DeKok was surprised. He had never heard a remark like that from the eccentric doctor.

"Why ... how so?" DeKok asked.

Dr. Koning removed his hat.

"Clowns with his talent are a rarity in our small country ... too valuable to murder indiscriminately."

He placed the Garibaldi hat in DeKok's hands and stepped onto the dock. Knees cracking, he knelt down next to the corpse. The investigation took longer than usual. Such an extended examination was rare. Once he'd finished, at least for the time being, the coroner rose, took off his pince-nez, and started polishing them with a large silk handkerchief he took from his breast pocket.

"He is dead," Koning said, as he replaced his glasses and handkerchief.

DeKok nodded.

"So I understood," he said.

Dr. Koning nodded in the direction of the corpse.

"He died at least six hours ago, perhaps longer. Rigor is complete."

He nodded once more at the corpse and then stretched out a hand to DeKok, who helped him board the launch.

"Internal bleeding?" asked DeKok.

The coroner gestured vaguely.

"Could be … I postulate internal bleeding may have led to the final demise. But the pathologist can give you a more precise answer after the autopsy."

He accepted his hat back from DeKok, placed it on his head, and carefully picked his way to the stern, where the same burly constable helped him back ashore. Once ashore he turned to DeKok.

"Ever seen a clown with no make-up?" he asked. Then he walked away.

DeKok pondered the question, but he did not have long. Weelen passed him on the way to the foredeck and Kruger, the dactyloscopist, asked what was expected from him.

"Everything on that little dock is wet," he complained,

"I can't get any prints."

DeKok made a careless gesture.

"Then don't. You're the expert. Whatever you think ..."

He did not finish his sentence, but pointed at the corpse. "I would like to have *his* fingerprints, though," he concluded.

Kruger looked at him.

"Right now?"

DeKok shook his head.

"No, you can do it tomorrow, before the autopsy."

Kruger gave him a grateful look.

When Kruger and Weelen had both left, DeKok waved over the morgue attendants.

"Transport him on his stomach," he warned. "Make sure to leave the knife in position for the lab."

The two men nodded simultaneously. They lifted the dead clown from the dock and placed him on the stretcher. Out of habit they draped a sheet over the corpse. Beneath the sheet the knife stood at an odd, almost comic, angle. Carefully they moved the stretcher to the quay.

DeKok stayed aft, observing the constables trying to keep onlookers at bay. Then he turned around, thanked the crew of the launch, and stepped onto the quay. He beckoned Vledder to follow. Vledder had just finished giving instructions for the taping of the crime scene and ensuring a uniformed constable would keep curiosity seekers out.

The two men were silent as they headed back to the station house. A human being had been horribly murdered. They were preoccupied with the thought of a murderer at large.

As they walked through the old quarter, DeKok looked around. The rhythm of the neighborhood had not been disturbed. Sleazy sex theaters did a brisk business. From the open door of a bar came the noise of stamping feet and the wail of an electric guitar. Some women giggled in front of the display window of a sex shop.

As they entered the station house, Jan Kuster, the watch commander, motioned them to approach the counter. As they stepped closer, Kuster looked at his notes.

"About half an hour ago we received a phone call from a Dongen, Peter Dongen. He's an impresario. He asked me to tell you that Pieter Eikelbos performs tonight in Groningen."

DeKok looked puzzled.

"Groningen" he repeated in a daze. Groningen is a city in the northern Netherlands. DeKok recalled, fleetingly, it was the birthplace of Mata Hari.

The watch commander nodded.

3

"He's performing as Pierrot ... the clown."

With his raincoat draped loosely across his wide shoulders, DeKok lowered himself in the chair behind his desk. His dilapidated little felt hat clung to the back of his head. The watch commander's voice still reverberated. He exchanged glances with Vledder, who looked at him despondently.

"Have you ever seen a clown without make-up?"

Vledder grimaced.

"I heard Dr. Koning asking you the same thing. It's a good question."

"Well?"

Vledder spread his hands in a helpless gesture.

"When does an ordinary person see a clown? Performing in a theater, in a circus, on television, but always *performing*. When I saw Pierrot in the theater, he had a chalk-white face with black circles around his eyes. I remember his appearance well. He was not just comical; he was a musical virtuoso. He played the flute, clarinet, and saxophone. Next he switched to the violin and the piano. Even the most gifted artists choose between groups of instruments. But his performance ran the gamut. It was a delight to hear and see. He was a phenomenal performer."

"And his face?"

Vledder showed impatience.

"I told you ... always made up. My seat was at least fifteen to twenty yards away from the stage. I recognized the clown on the dock as Pierrot by his clothing. Every clown has unique make-up and dress. Clowns register their stage personas. You will never see two clowns dressed and made up the same ... so I understand." He paused thoughtfully. "When I saw the body," he continued, "he was on his stomach. Later, once he was on the stretcher, I was able to get a better look at the face." He sighed deeply. "It didn't do anything for me. It was the face of a stranger. He was maybe forty, forty-five years old."

DeKok rubbed his little finger along the bridge of his nose.

"So," he said with a sigh, "we now have two Pierrots. One is alive and well in Groningen and another is on a slab."

Vledder nodded somberly.

"Which is the real one?"

DeKok pursed his lips before answering.

"This shouldn't be tough. If the performer in Groningen displays the musical virtuosity of the man who performed in the Variety Revue, *he* is legitimate." He paused and rubbed his chin. "Unless ... unless, one believes two people could possess such musical expertise. Even if that were true, someone would have had to see Pierrot's act often enough to be able to mimic it." He stretched out a finger toward Vledder. "Just as you recognized Pierrot by his costume, the audience in Groningen could be fooled by the substance of the performance."

Vledder gave his mentor a long, thoughtful look.

"You actually mean," he said hesitantly, "just about anybody could be hiding behind the costume and make-up in Groningen."

"Something like that."

He stared into the distance.

"And perhaps the real Pierrot is now waiting on a cold table in the pathology lab."

DeKok thought. He was momentarily overwhelmed with possibilities.

"Of one thing I am sure," he said with a sigh, "we've entered a maze."

Slowly he came to his feet, stretched, and walked over to the peg on the wall to hang his raincoat and his hat.

"Why don't you concoct some sort of preliminary report for the commissaris," he said as he walked back to his desk. "You know how he feels about being kept in the loop. As soon as he has drunk his first cup of coffee, he'll start fussing about being the last to know *anything*."

Vledder grinned as he pulled the keyboard of his computer closer.

"A preliminary report," he murmured. "I haven't done many of those. What do you want to put in it?"

DeKok stood next to Vledder's desk.

"Inspectors Vledder and DeKok," he dictated, "report that—fill in today's date—at 21:15 hours, a body was discovered on a wooden dock at the feet of The Criers' Tower. The body was that of an unknown male, dressed in a clown's costume. Apparently the man was killed with a large throwing knife, which was stuck in the back of the victim."

Vledder looked up.

"A throwing knife?"

DeKok nodded.

"Exactly. It was the type of knife professional carnies throw at attractive female assistants on stage."

"I didn't notice," said Vledder. "It was a rather large knife of a peculiar shape. I should have gone a step further." He pushed his keyboard away. "Could the killer have thrown the knife from a distance?"

DeKok shrugged.

"Perhaps you should discuss that with Dr. Rusteloos tomorrow, before the autopsy. He could have seen something like it before. Maybe the wound will tell him how it was—" DeKok suddenly stopped talking. The door to the detective room opened and a man stuck his head around the door.

"Come in," called Vledder.

The man entered fully. He was athletic looking, lean and lithe, with remarkable white-blond hair. DeKok figured him to be in his late twenties. He was dressed in gray slacks and a blue blazer with an anchor emblem on the breast pocket. He approached the two inspectors with the gait of a gymnast. He stretched out a hand.

"You're Inspector DeKok?"

"With a kay-oh-kay," said DeKok automatically, shaking hands.

The young man smiled, showing a set of strong, white teeth.

"My name is Maurice ... Maurice Vlaanderen. My father was here earlier this evening."

DeKok smiled.

"With a story about an extraordinary theft," he commented and pointed to a chair next to his desk. "Are you here to tell me the jewels have been found?"

Maurice Vlaanderen shook his head.

"You are our only hope." He sank down in the offered chair. "You have a great reputation as a sleuth. So they say."

DeKok grinned.

"Give *them* my regards," he said dryly.

The young man's face became more thoughtful.

"Seriously, Inspector DeKok, I would be so grateful if you could solve this strange theft. We're not so worried about the money. According to our lawyer, the insurance company will eventually pay the damages. It isn't only because of the irreplaceable nature of the jewels, either." He hesitated a moment. "It is because of my father."

DeKok pensively pulled on his earlobe as he studied the young man.

"What's the matter with your father?"

Maurice seemed to search for words.

"Let me see how to put this. He has been a changed man since the theft. I hardly recognize my father. Like most people, he has suffered setbacks in his lifetime. He's absorbed some serious shocks, but he has always managed to hit the ground running."

DeKok shrugged.

"He made a normal impression upon me."

Young Vlaanderen smiled indulgently.

"Father was very much impressed by you. In fact, he was surprised you accepted his strange story. That is to say, you gave him that impression."

DeKok leaned his head to one side.

"But he spoke the truth."

Maurice Vlaanderen gesticulated wildly, his face red and his nostrils quivering.

"That's exactly the problem," he cried out. "It is he who cannot accept the truth. He refuses to believe the jewels disappeared from the safe. He doesn't want to discuss it, but keeps harping about a loss of memory. Tomorrow he has an appointment with a psychiatrist."

DeKok seemed surprised.

"Is that a first?"

"Yes."

"Why?"

Maurice released a deep sigh.

"Fear. His memory has always been sharp. He's afraid it's the beginning of some debilitating or degenerative disease."

DeKok shook his head.

"Your father is a long way from that," he said soothingly. "There appeared to me to be no dementia. I'm sure there will be an explanation for the vanishing jewels." He smiled. "We simply don't have the explanation right now." With both hands DeKok pressed his body in a more upright position, clearly indicating that this was the end of the interview. "Give my regards to your father."

Vlaanderen did not get up.

"There's something else," he said timidly, "Father did not want to tell you."

"What's that, then?"

The young man stood up and looked DeKok straight in the eye.

"Butterfly."

Vledder slapped himself on the thighs from pure exhilaration within moments after Maurice Vlaanderen had left.

"Butterfly," he laughed. "Butterfly. The only thing the man can remember after the theft of millions, is 'butterfly.' He's an original, alright. He must have been thinking of the little butterfly that spent the night."

DeKok ignored his colleague's outburst. He did not find "butterfly" all that comical. He appreciated the remarks of the broker, but wondered how he could transform the single word into a concept. DeKok needed any lead during this phase of his investigation. He suspected the word stuck in the senior Vlaanderen's subconscious for a reason. But finding the connection between this single word and a mysterious theft would be quite another matter.

He looked at Vledder, who was calming down, but there was still a grin on his face and his eyes twinkled.

"Have you sent the APB?"

"What APB?"

"The one describing the jewels."

The last signs of amusement disappeared from Vledder's face. He pulled the keyboard of his computer closer and touched the keys.

"Yes and no," he said. "Here is the report and the description of the jewelry. It hasn't gone out yet."

"Well, hadn't you better do that? And don't forget to add a note about the butterfly bit."

"Yes, of course," said Vledder and performed the necessary commands on his keyboard.

DeKok shook his head. In the old days he would have delivered a handwritten report to the typing room. An old, grizzled constable, no longer fit for street duty, would have used two fingers to prepare a punch tape from the written text for the telex. Similar punch tapes would spit out at all police stations. Other grizzled constables would laboriously decode the tapes into legible reports. These would be typed onto stencils by means of manual typewriters. Then the reports would be mimeographed for distribution throughout the various precincts. DeKok was satisfied. From his viewpoint, no further technological advance was required.

"Did you mention the butterfly thing?" he asked.

"Yes," said Vledder, still flustered over his own procrastination.

"Good."

DeKok took a telephone directory from a drawer in his desk and looked for the name "Dongen."

He found the address and stood up. As he struggled into his raincoat, Vledder asked what he was up to.

"We're going to Willem Park Way," answered DeKok, as he put his hat on. "We need to ask an impresario how well he knows his clowns."

Peter Dongen, the impresario and manager of artists, was a tall, broad-shouldered man with a full head of wavy hair. His steel-blue eyes were set in a sharp, angular, tan face. His wide, dimpled chin jutted aggressively. He strode ahead of the inspectors to a large space, dominated by an oversized, disorderly desk. With a wave of his hands he invited his visitors to an alcove furnished with a table and modern, steel chairs.

"Please have a seat," he said. His voice was deep and warm. "How may I help you gentlemen?"

DeKok sat down and placed his hat on the floor next to his chair.

"Sir," he began hesitantly, "we are charged with investigating the death of a clown."

With a smile, Dongen interrupted him.

"You're talking about the man in the clown's costume?"

DeKok nodded.

"That's one way to put it." He pointed at Vledder. "My colleague seems to recall the man as Pierrot, a musical clown. He thoroughly enjoyed a performance in the Municipal

Theater last year. I also understand you called our station house to tell us Pierrot was performing in Groningen tonight."

Peter Dongen crossed his long legs.

"Yes, I received a call from the manager of the Municipal Theater," he explained. "Old man Willink. A rather upsetting phone call, I should add. He wanted to know what was wrong with Pierrot."

"And?"

The impresario grinned.

"I told him nothing was going on with Pierrot. I told him about the performance in Groningen. Then Mr. Willink told me to call Warmoes Street Station, because they had reported Pierrot dead."

DeKok nodded his understanding.

"We have a request for you," he said in an official tone of voice. "We want you to identify our dead Pierrot."

Dongen's face fell.

"When?"

"Now."

Dongen looked at his watch.

"But it's almost midnight," he protested.

DeKok gave him a long, expressionless look.

"What better time to visit a morgue?"

Dongen rode in the cramped back seat of the old VW Beetle, his displeasure showing. They made their way from his office to the morgue, which was attached to the pathology lab. Vledder, as usual, was driving and DeKok was slouched down in the passenger seat. His little hat was pushed down over his eyes and he seemed asleep.

Their reluctant passenger had exhausted his reasons not to go. In the end he caved to DeKok's quiet insistence. The prospect of having to face death kept him silent during the ride.

On arrival at the morgue, Vledder produced the key to the forecourt gate. He drove through the gate, parking at the base of the stairway leading to the front door. An old watchman appeared. Recognizing both inspectors he continued on his rounds. They climbed the steps and entered. Only the click of their footsteps echoed down the long, partially lit hallway. The morgue and pathology lab were at the end of the hall. Here bodies awaited either burial or autopsy. The place was cold, and a pall of silence hung over it.

"Nine to five sounding better?" asked Vledder idly, as he glanced back down the deserted corridor.

DeKok shook his head in disapproval. He didn't want to hear it just now. There were simply not enough murders in Amsterdam to warrant perpetual staffing.

Vledder sauntered to the wall where banks of drawers contained the deceased. He proceeded to read labels and opened a drawer. As the drawer slid out on well-oiled rollers, he flicked the sheet back from over the head. Pierrot was still on his stomach, the knife still protruding from his back. But his head had been turned to one side, to make the face visible. Death presented itself in the harsh neon light in its most revolting aspect.

Dongen, who had followed Vledder, took a frightened step back when he saw the face. With a shaking hand he pointed at the corpse.

"This is impossible! This isn't happening. It isn't true … it isn't true," he repeated. "I telephoned Groningen myself."

DeKok looked grim.

"What isn't true," he asked.

Peter Dongen lowered his head and sobbed.

"It *is* our Pierrot."

4

"Pieter Eikelbos?"

The impresario did not answer. With a look of disbelief he stared at the corpse. Then he paled and began to reel.

DeKok hastened forward and signaled Vledder. The young inspector covered the face and pushed back the drawer into the wall. DeKok was familiar with the symptoms. He was afraid that the tall impresario would faint on the spot and he quickly led him outside.

The fresh night air revived Dongen a bit. He took a few deep breaths and regained some color in his face. DeKok gave him a thoughtful look.

"Was that Pieter Eikelbos?"

Dongen nodded slowly.

"Pieter Eikelbos was his real name. Pierre was his child-hood nickname, given to him by his parents. That's why he chose Pierrot as his professional name." He shook his head in despair and sighed deeply. "It is … unimaginable."

"What?"

"Pierre is there, in that drawer. Had I not seen it with my own eyes …" Dongen did not finish the sentence. He lowered his head and stared at the ground. "Poor Pierre was always sad beneath his surface. Depression is the occupational disease of clowns." There was a pleasant, almost wistful timbre to his voice, but suddenly his tone changed. "This I cannot comprehend," he said sharply. "When Willink called to tell me his distressing news, I immediately called the theater in Groningen. They assured me Pierrot had performed. He was on the program just before the intermission. The performance was, as ever, a great success."

DeKok pointed at the closed door of the morgue building.

"But it wasn't Pierrot," he said. His manner was laconic. "We have established a time of death. *This* Pierrot was dead for more then six hours before we found him. Therefore the question remains, *which* Pierrot performed in Groningen?"

Peter Dongen shook his head vehemently.

"This is surreal."

DeKok smiled gently.

"But it happened. You checked it yourself."

The impresario shook himself, as if trying to shake off the truth.

"No, I tell you. Pierre's act was unique. He was a grand performer, a veteran of many years. He continually polished his act, never taking his success for granted. Pierre was a perfectionist, always in rehearsal. His profession was his life; there was nothing else for him."

"Are you familiar with his act?"

Peter Dongen nodded with emphasis.

"I can recall every movement, every tone of his instruments. I must have seen his performance at least thirty times over the years. He continued to astonish audiences, who found every performance spellbinding. He had true comedic range, from slapstick to sentimental to melancholy. Only he could perform that way."

"Inimitable?"

"Absolutely."

Vledder wished the old watchman goodnight, and returned to them. DeKok had a puzzled look.

"You took your time."

"I took another look at the knife."

"And?"

"You're right ... it's a knife designed for throwing."

Peter Dongen reacted frightened.

"Why do you say it was designed for throwing," he cried out with apprehension. "What made you think that?"

Vledder looked from the impresario to DeKok and back again.

After a moment's hesitation, he said, "It was a knife such as a carnie knife thrower uses."

Dongen swallowed.

"And that's what ... killed Pierre?"

DeKok nodded.

"We're certain. Of course the autopsy will confirm the cause of death. The knife is still in his back."

Peter Dongen closed his eyes.

"Fantinelli."

DeKok frowned.

"Who or what is Fantinelli?"

"He has a knife-throwing act." The impresario covered his eyes with both hands. "He threatened several times to go after Pierre with a knife."

DeKok hopped off the streetcar he was riding. He ambled along the wide sidewalk of the Damrak, hands thrust deep into the pockets of his raincoat. There was a relaxed grin on his face. The sunshine and fresh air were so enticing, he'd diverted from his usual route via New Bridge Alley.

Now he was following the stream of pedestrians along the Damrak. Amsterdam was not a city built for cars. It was a haven for pedestrians and cyclists. DeKok recalled how, years before, an enterprising tourist bureau had organized a walking tour of Amsterdam. The entire tour took less than a morning. In addition to the old police station at Warmoes Street, there were fifty-some tourist attractions. Where else in the world could one pass Anne Frank's house, Rembrandt's house, picturesque bridges, a restaurant as wide as a VW, and The Criers' Tower? All were within easy walking distance from each other. The same tour by car, DeKok reflected, would probably take all day, maybe longer.

He pushed his hat farther back on his head and looked up. The flags on the docks of the sightseeing boats waved gaily in the slight breeze under a cloudless sky. On the other side of the water he saw Warmoes Street in shadows. In the office of the commissaris he could just discern the silhouette of the tall Commissaris Buitendam, his chief and nemesis. DeKok suppressed the urge to jump up and down and wave to attract his attention. It was hard to resist. He continued walking, a naughty grin on his face. The uptight commissaris would deplore a public display.

On the corner of Old Bridge Alley a barrel organ played "La Vie en Rose." What an appropriate tune for a day like today, thought DeKok. Certainly this was a day to see through rose-colored glasses. He searched his pockets. Among the toffees, peppermints, and other assorted candy, he found a coin. He threw it in the direction of the man who accompanied the organ. With a practiced gesture the man caught the coin in his cap. He nodded at DeKok and DeKok smiled back.

He crossed the Damrak and looked with pleasure at the old Stock Exchange building. A recent cleaning left the facade looking brand new. He started to hum a Christmas carol and nodded to a working girl he had known for years. Despite her provocative clothing, she was obviously not working. Like DeKok, she was simply enjoying the glorious day.

DeKok was happy. Yes, there was yet another nasty, complicated murder. He chose this life when he chose his strange profession. His old mother chided him for not learning a trade. She always insisted he needed something to "fall back on." She never really approved of her son's choice of work. She did not want any child of hers exposed to the criminal element, to say nothing of the *danger*.

He greeted the watch commander enthusiastically as he entered the lobby of the station house. On the worn stairs he encountered Vledder, who was leaving.

"Where are you headed?"

"To the autopsy," explained Vledder. "I'm already late. I should have been there at ten."

DeKok nodded his understanding.

"Give Dr. Rusteloos my regards. When you get back we'll discuss this Fantinelli. And please bring the knife back from the morgue."

Vledder took the rest of the stairs in a rush, but at the bottom he turned around.

"Commissaris Buitendam has asked for you," he called back up the stairs.

"Was our preliminary report too preliminary?" asked DeKok with a grin.

"I don't know. He said nothing about the report. He just told me to send you to his room when you came in."

Commissaris Buitendam indicated the chair in front of his desk with a narrow, elegant hand.

"Please, sit down, DeKok," he said in his pompous voice. "I wish to be further informed."

The old sleuth had a truculent look as he took the seat. He would have preferred to stand. He felt more in command of the situation that way. A summons to meetings with the commissaris always raised his suspicions. He instinctively protected the autonomy of his office. This led to self-assertion.

The happiness he had felt at the beginning of the glorious day was waning. It flowed from him like water draining out of a bathtub. His exuberance was being replaced by irked annoyance.

"Was our report not clear enough?" he asked.

Buitendam looked a bit sheepish.

"What report?"

"We reported the murder of a clown."

The commissaris coughed discreetly.

"Yes, yes, it is such a strange case. We'll have to dispose of it somehow."

DeKok swallowed.

"Do something about it," he corrected him. "It's murder, a foul, well-planned, murder."

Buitendam raised his left hand, stretched his chin, and rubbed his neck with the tops of his thumb and fingers. It was a familiar gesture, meant to gain time. DeKok cocked his head and stared at the commissaris.

"About what," he asked, "do you want to be informed?"

The commissaris coughed again.

"Last night a certain Julius Vlaanderen came to see you

in reference to the theft of a considerable amount of antique jewelry from his safe."

DeKok nodded.

"Indeed. I read the rather strange story. But I fear I will have little time to spend on it. The murder of the clown has certain aspects—"

Buitendam waved him into silence.

"The theft from Vlaanderen is not an isolated case. There have been more of these rather puzzling thefts involving mysterious disappearances of jewelry and money."

DeKok shrugged.

"I had not heard about that," he said carelessly.

Buitendam nodded.

"The other cases happened in The Hague. The victims were important people. Their attorneys went directly to the attorney general. In the interests of the victims, the attorney general's office felt the reports should not be made public."

DeKok was stunned.

"Why not?"

"It is simply a matter of policy."

DeKok grinned.

"My policy is to find the thief and return the stolen property," he mocked. "An APB went out."

Buitendam nodded again.

"Exactly. Your APB disturbed a hornet's nest in The Hague."

Now DeKok looked down.

"But why? It was just a routine report."

"From your report, investigators in The Hague have connected the Vlaanderen case with theirs."

"What's the connection?"

The commissaris tapped his finger on the report on his desk.

"Little butterfly … the only thing the victims in The Hague remember about the thefts is that. Your APB mentioned that the word or name "butterfly" was the only clue to a possible perpetrator."

DeKok smirked, remembering Vledder's reaction. Apparently he had changed his opinion by the end of the report. DeKok seldom read the reports.

"And that," said DeKok, "caused the attorney general in his upscale Hague office such an upset. He couldn't bring himself to entrust the information to a telex."

Although Amsterdam is the capitol of the Netherlands, the government resides in The Hague. This strikes a sour note with true Amsterdammers, who consider the remainder of the Netherlands the Hinterlands."

A red spot roughly the size of a ping-pong ball appeared on each commissarial cheek.

"He was acting on the purest of motives. The attorney general did not want the integrity of the victims open to question."

This time DeKok laughed heartily.

"Their integrity won't bear the weight of a *little butterfly?*" He stood up. "How about this—we'll send all the details of the Vlaanderen case to The Hague. To avoid further embarrassment to a few socialites, they can handle all the cases. What's the name of the judge advocate in The Hague? Or do I send it directly to the attorney general?" With a grin he rubbed the back of his neck. "Then their secret will be safe and the little butterfly no longer a pest."

Buitendam's face fell. He licked his dry lips and swallowed before he spoke again.

"Early this morning ..." he began slowly, "early this morning The Hague contacted *our* judge advocate, Mr. Schaap. He wishes you to assume responsibility for The Hague's cases."

DeKok looked as if he had been hit with a hammer.

"What!?" he roared. "The stuffed shirts in The Hague are so busy schmoozing and kissing up they can't get hold of the case? So they'd like us to get our hands dirty?" He shook his head resolutely. "I don't think so. I have a murder on my hands."

Buitendam also came out of his chair.

"Mr. Schaap wants—"

DeKok interrupted him.

"You tell Mr. Schaap a man's life is more important than jewelry collectors with their pants down. Tell him, in this case, I set my own priorities."

The commissaris was literally seething with anger. His face turned red and his hands balled into fists. Then he stretched an arm out to the door.

"OUT!!"

DeKok left.

When Vledder returned from the autopsy, he found his old colleague sitting at his desk. Vledder smiled when he saw the look on DeKok's face.

"Meeting go well, as usual?"

DeKok nodded. He was still heavily offended and it showed.

"It's too crazy for words," he said. "Buitendam has a judge-advocate complex. Is it fear or is he just a career boot-licker, take your pick. Maybe it really is the way to the top.

Schaap calls him about Vlaanderen and the jewels, all of a sudden everything else is out the window. He was dismissive when it came to the savage murder of a clown."

Vledder shook his head.

"Come on. You're holding out, what else happened?"

DeKok told the rest. Vledder listened calmly, but when DeKok mentioned the butterfly, he sat up.

"Well, it seems clear," he said finally, "it's our own fault. We should never have said anything about that. It's why we have all this trouble."

DeKok slammed his fist on the desk.

"But it means something," he said angrily. "That's now obvious."

"But what?"

DeKok did not answer right away. His anger was ebbing. The next time he spoke, his expression and tone were milder.

"Let The Hague figure it out. Isn't that why they have super powers?" He shook his head as if to clear it. "How was the autopsy?" he asked. "Was there internal bleeding?"

Vledder nodded.

"Dr. Rusteloos was unable to tell whether the knife had been pushed or thrown. According to him, the effect on the body would be roughly the same. But it must have entered into the body with some force. The knife grazed a rib and severed an artery."

"He died of internal hemorrhage?"

"Right."

"Did you bring the weapon?"

Vledder removed the wrapping from the package on his desk. He then lifted the heavy knife in his hand.

"I spoke again with the fingerprint experts. They still

have no usable prints, which leaves only dried blood samples they took for analysis. They'll get back to us."

The phone on DeKok's desk rang. Vledder leaned over and lifted it from the cradle. He listened for a moment and then turned to DeKok.

"Fantinelli is downstairs. They're asking what to do with him?"

5

DeKok rubbed his face with both hands. Then he looked at Vledder through his spread fingers.

"He can go to the waiting room, for the time being. Just tell them we'll collect him in a few minutes." He raised a finger in the air. "By all means he is not to leave."

Vledder relayed the instructions and replaced the receiver.

"Why do you think he's here?"

DeKok stretched out a hand toward the knife.

"Just give me that."

Vledder handed him the knife.

"Do you think he knows?" asked Vledder.

"What?"

"That the clown was killed with a throwing knife?"

DeKok closed his eyes for a moment.

"What did it say in the papers?"

"There was nothing about the murder weapon. I looked through two morning papers. Both reported it in a short notice, somewhere inside the paper. Just the bare facts, 'Dead clown found near The Criers' Tower.' That was it. No name and no further particulars."

"It's been a while since a murder was front-page news."

It sounded bitter and cynical. Then he realized the evening papers were ready in distribution before the ghastly discovery. The morning papers were probably in their first press run. Removal of the remains had gone relatively quickly and quietly.

He rubbed the bridge of his nose with his little finger. It took a while before he spoke again.

"If," he said slowly, "if Fantinelli knows about the knife, there are two possibilities. Either Peter Dongen told him, or he is the killer. Let us hear his story."

Vledder went downstairs to the waiting room and led the man upstairs to the detective room. He motioned to a chair next to DeKok's desk and unobtrusively retired to his own desk. He turned on his computer to make notes. DeKok noticed with approval that he also placed his notebook on the desk. Vledder knew DeKok trusted handwritten notes more than anything entered directly on a computer.

The gray sleuth turned to the visitor and smiled amicably.

"My name is DeKok ... with a kay-oh-kay." He pointed at Vledder. "And this is my colleague, Detective Vledder, whom you already met."

The man nodded. He glanced at Vledder and then turned back toward DeKok.

"I read in the paper you found a dead clown at the foot of Criers' Tower."

"That is correct."

"I want to see him."

DeKok feigned surprise.

"Why?"

The man moved in his chair and then leaned aggressively forward.

"I want to know who it is," he said curtly, with a sharp

overtone. "It could be anybody." He gesticulated. "What is a clown? A clown is nothing ... absolutely nothing ... a crazy costume, big shoes, and a snoot full of paint."

DeKok listened carefully to both the tone and the content of the words. The undertone gave DeKok a sense of more than professional jealousy or contempt. This grudge was personal. He leaned back in his chair and gave the visitor his policeman's stare. He saw a round face and a black, slightly receding hairline. Brown eyes gleamed malevolently under heavy, bristling eyebrows.

DeKok leaned forward again.

"I don't seem to remember," he said evenly, "you introducing yourself."

The man pointed at the floor.

"Downstairs at the counter, I told them I am Fantinelli."

DeKok nodded.

"Fantinelli," he repeated slowly. "It sounds Italian. Is it your family name?"

The man shook his head.

"It's my stage name. My real name is Kees Kappelhof," he smiled sadly. "You understand ... not exactly the name for a poster."

DeKok smiled politely.

"You're a performing artist?" he asked superfluously.

"Yes ... variety ... knife thrower."

DeKok gave his visitor a look full of admiration.

"I've been a fan of theater since my early childhood," he lied with conviction. "It's a love I inherited from my father. I am particularly taken by knife-throwing acts. They, you, have it all—courage, power, precision. I am an aficionado." He cocked his head. "And you work with a beautiful woman on the turning wheel?"

"Yes, my wife."

"Tell me, are you never afraid you'll miss?"

Fantinelli shook his head.

"No, but maybe I'll miss one day."

DeKok shook his head, as if to wake himself.

"I don't follow."

The knife thrower moved in his chair again. His face turned red and there again was an angry look on his face.

"The bitch works every room, flirts with every new guy. She's on the make and on the move, flitting from one to another like a nympho. The newest heartthrob is a clown."

DeKok feigned surprise.

"A clown you say?"

"Yes."

DeKok suddenly pointed a finger at Fantinelli.

"That's why you want to see the dead clown," he said as if it was a revelation.

Fantinelli nodded emphatically.

"Yes, if he's dead, we'll have peace for a while."

Suddenly DeKok's affable manner changed. His tone became sharp and incisive.

"When *who* is dead?"

The knife thrower did not answer.

"When *who* is dead?" repeated DeKok, insistently.

Fantinelli lowered his head.

"Pierrot."

Vledder was shaken.

His voice cracked in astonishment and anger, "You let him go? You just let him go!" He pointed both arms at the door of the detective room. "Just like that ... the murderer walks."

DeKok shook his head.

"He's not the murderer."

Vledder grimaced, disbelief on his face.

"He has a clear motive." He gestured toward the throwing knife on DeKok's desk. "And that thing in Pierrot's back was *his* knife."

DeKok slid the weapon back in his desk drawer.

"He admitted as much," he said calmly. "But a complete set of knives was stolen from his car in Amersfoort last month. The local police investigated the incident. You made the call—did they not confirm it?"

Vledder smiled crookedly.

"It proves nothing," he exclaimed. "Somehow I think Fantinelli is smart enough to report his knives stolen as a smokescreen."

DeKok sighed deeply.

"He simply did not do it."

Vledder gesticulated wildly. Never before had he been in more disagreement with his mentor.

"And we know that because ..." he asked sarcastically.

"I have a gut feeling."

For a moment the young inspector closed his eyes, as if praying for strength.

"Now we're going on intuition," he said dully. "We need proof to eliminate him as a suspect." He turned his chair around and straddled it backward.

"Can't you see some logic in this, DeKok?" he asked, more reasonably.

"What?"

"Despite his obvious boldness, Fantinelli is by no means a clever man. Right after the killing he makes a beeline for the police to announce his motive."

"Yes, so what?"

Vledder snorted. DeKok was being especially obtuse.

"We'd be unlikely to miss the affair between Fantinelli's wife and Pierrot in the course of our investigation. By artlessly telling us that, he took the wind out of our sails."

DeKok rubbed the corners of his eyes with his fingers. It was a tired gesture. He turned toward Vledder and placed a hand on the young man's shoulder.

"Listen, Dick," he said patiently, "Fantinelli has no real motive. Nothing. Apparently his wife has had relations with several men over the years. He knew about the affairs. Nothing ever came of the liaisons. The acrobat still performs his caprioles, fit as a fiddle. The trapeze artist still flies far above the crowd."

Vledder wasn't about to drop it.

"Nonetheless the *clown* is dead."

DeKok gave his young colleague a tired smile.

"Indeed," he said evenly. "By a knife, but not by the knife thrower. What are the chances he'd be stupid enough to use one of his own knives to kill a rival?" DeKok stood up. "Look, in spite of it all, the guy loves his wife. He isn't prepared to lose her forever. She's gotten away with these 'escapades' for years. She remains under his wing, regardless of the occasional confrontation. Now, suddenly, he ..." He did not finish the sentence. Slowly he walked over to the peg where he kept his raincoat and his hat.

Vledder followed. His mentor had still not convinced him.

"Where are you going?"

DeKok grinned.

"I'm going to see Little Lowee. I feel the need for a bracing glass of cognac."

Lowee's real name was Louis, yet because of his diminutive size he was known as Little Lowee. Lowee's mousy face changed to an expression of joy when he saw DeKok and Vledder enter the dark, intimate bar. He stopped the rinsing of some glasses, dried his hands quickly on his vest, and reached out a hand to the inspector. He shook hands enthusiastically. Vledder received a condescending nod.

"Well come," he chirped, "welcome, Negozie."

Negozie is an underworld word for "business" or "establishment." Lowee spoke a type of Dutch that even native Dutchmen found hard to understand. His language was the language of the underworld and the gutter. A mixture of several languages with meanings far removed from their original intent and almost all mispronounced. The closest thing to Bargoens, as it is called, would probably be a mixture of Cockney, Yiddish, Dutch, and Papiamento, which is itself a mixture of Dutch, Portuguese, and several African dialects.

DeKok was the only cop in the Netherlands who both understood and spoke Bargoens, but he firmly refused to speak it.

"And a good afternoon to you," said DeKok.

"So, whatsa going atta station?" asked Lowee.

Without waiting for an answer the small barkeeper placed three snifters on the counter and then produced a bottle of fine French cognac. The label on the dusty, amber bottle belonged to a respected vintner. With an almost devout gesture he held the bottle up for DeKok to see.

"From the ol' supply, yet," Lowee said with a satisfied smile. "I'm more careful widdit then m' wife, if I had one."

With an expert movement he removed the cork and

carefully poured the golden liquid in the waiting glasses. His movements had the appearance of a solemn ceremony.

DeKok watched with a friendly, anticipatory smile on his face. He loved these moments. He was fully aware that Lowee was both a thief and a fence, a man who had broken just about every law and commandment. DeKok did not judge the small barkeep. Their unlikely friendship had grown into mutual love and respect.

"Proost," said DeKok, as he lifted his glass. Lowee and Vledder followed suit.

DeKok rocked the glass slowly in his hand and then sniffed the aroma of the truly exceptional drink. Then he took a careful sip. Softly the velvet drink slid down his throat. He gave the glass a long look and took another sip. Then he replaced the glass on the bar.

"There are moments," he said, "when I am completely at peace with the universe. This is one of those moments."

Lowee nodded in agreement.

"Couldna said it better m'self," he said. "You gotta way wiv words."

Vledder snorted.

"You don't spend all day with him."

Lowee did not even turn his head toward the young inspector. He still had trouble accepting Vledder as a worthy patron. He tolerated the man because of his association with DeKok. As if Vledder had not been there, Lowee repeated his original question.

"So, whazzup atta station?" he asked.

DeKok smiled.

"We won't be jobless anytime soon. There's no crime recession." He leaned closer across the bar. "I'm looking for antique jewels," he whispered.

"A lot?"

"Worth about a million."

Lowee whistled between his teeth in appreciation.

"Thassa haul," he said with admiration. "Good stuff?"

"I think so. If it happens to be offered ... you know where I am."

Lowee looked doubtful.

"They ain't gonna see me. Don't go for jools. Too easy to spot and there ain't no green in fox."

Vledder wanted to know what "fox" was. DeKok explained it was the catch-all phrase for melted down gold and silver jewelry removed from its mountings. Even Vledder knew that "green" meant money.

DeKok changed the subject.

"Ever hear of a Clarisse?" he asked. "She is a working girl, associated with an escort service."

Lowee winked.

"Carol Ponytail."

"Is that her real name?"

The barkeeper grinned.

"I know she use Clarisse as a moniker. To me she's just Carol. Ever since she were a kid, she done her hair in a ponytail. Silly Kate will have her address."

DeKok nodded his thanks and drained his glass.

"Why don't you pour one for the road."

Lowee responded with alacrity.

"Is them dead clown one of youse, too?"

DeKok smiled.

"You mean, am I handling the case?"

Lowee nodded.

"You been seen at the weep stick."

"That's right," laughed DeKok. He thought "weep stick"

was an original name for The Criers' Tower. "Did you hear anything?"

Lowee grinned.

"Plenty street rumers."

"What sort of rumors?" prompted DeKok.

"They was busted."

DeKok looked puzzled.

"Who was bankrupt?"

"Them variety group."

"You mean the clown at Criers' Tower was part of a group that went bankrupt?"

"Yep."

"How big is that group?"

"Oh about ten, maybe a dozen of them guys."

"No women?"

Lowee laughed.

"Of course they got bints. Variety wiv' no bints ... no way. Good lookin' broads. They been here a few times when they's in Mokum." He turned to Vledder and said in perfectly accented Dutch: "That is Amsterdam to you." He then resumed in his usual gutter language. "Like most of them showbiz folk, they stops by ... after the show." He lost himself in thought. "Yeah," he added, "good-lookin' broads ... Butterfly was a babe."

DeKok almost choked on his cognac.

"Butterfly?"

Little Lowee nodded emphatically.

"Exacto. She danced wiv' them plastic wings on her back. She sorta floated onna cable over the stage. Crowd ate it up."

DeKok replaced his glass.

"Butterfly," he whispered in amazement. "Butterfly."

With a sudden upsurge of affection he took Lowee's small face between his hands.

"Lowee," he said tenderly, "sometimes you too have a way with words."

6

The inspectors found their way from Lowee's to Rear Fort Canal. They ambled in the direction of Old Acquaintance Alley. A steady drizzle raised a gray, damp veil over the canals. Business was as brisk as usual in the quarter. Crowds of tourists in crumpled plastic paraded along the streets and canals. Prostitutes displayed themselves behind the windows. People formed a queue at a sex theater.

DeKok pulled up the collar of his raincoat and pushed his hat farther forward. A young, beautiful, heroin whore took him by the arm. She had a dark, troubled look in her eyes and her hair was plastered around her head.

"Do you want to do it?" she asked.

DeKok looked at her.

"What?" he asked puzzled, his thoughts miles away.

She shook her head. The troubled look in her eyes disappeared for a moment.

"If I have to explain," she said, with pity in her voice, "you're too old to need it."

With a grin she slipped away and disappeared in the crowd.

Vledder burst out laughing.

"You see, they all think you're decrepit."

DeKok shrugged it off, but the incident saddened him. This skinny, disheveled girl had no clue DeKok was an officer of the law. Her boldness betrayed her naïveté. She couldn't have worked these streets long. She had likely just arrived in the quarter. He was struck by the influx of ever-younger prostitutes. They were children, abandoned by everyone, lost in hard-core addiction. After all, soft drugs were readily available in coffee shops, even from certain government outlets. When Holland decriminalized drug use, the number of new addicts plummeted by nearly ninety percent. Strangely this success did not translate to a reduction in the number of heroin prostitutes, quite the contrary. DeKok could not reconcile it. He was not alone.

From Old Acquaintance Alley they crossed the bridge to Old Church Square. At Saint Anna Alley, DeKok pushed open a green entry. Vledder followed, hoisting his weight up the narrow, steep stairs.

"Why are we here?" he asked.

The old man kept his momentum.

"We're going to see if Silly Kate is awake."

On the second floor landing DeKok tried the front door of an apartment. The door was not locked. It opened into a small kitchen. The next room was a living room.

In an easy chair, her corpulent body wrapped in a silk kimono embroidered with red, fire-spitting dragons, they found Silly Kate reading a magazine. She looked comical with half-glasses at the tip of her nose, her hair in pink curlers.

The unexpected arrival of the men did not disturb her equilibrium. Calmly she put the magazine down, took off her glasses, and looked up. When she recognized DeKok, she grinned.

"Hello, you old rat catcher."

DeKok smiled back.

"We just stopped by to see if you were awake."

"I've been awake since before I woke up. I've been wide awake all my life."

DeKok thumbed in the direction of Vledder.

"You know him?"

Kate nodded slowly.

"The new wave," she said with disapproval in her voice. "I wonder what they'll ever contribute."

"What do you mean?"

She shrugged.

"Ach, old workhorses like you understand people. These brash, young cops may be bright ..." She did not finish the sentence, but waved a plump arm at the window. "Just look outside. Girls used to play with dolls at that age. Now they play a deadly game." She shook her head. "I remember a time when the cops would have had them in custody within days. Sounds harsh—it *was* harsh. At least jail was a place to get clean, maybe live a little longer. These kids are standing in front of the graves they dig themselves, while we look the other way. Nobody cares enough to give them a running start."

DeKok remained silent. He found it curious the oldsters cared about the heroin problem, but it was the youngsters who were dying. There had to be, he thought, a reason.

Silly Kate looked up at him and studied the thoughtful look on his face.

"So why are you standing there like somebody who's been caught with his hand in the cookie jar?" Her tone was suddenly sharp and accusing. "You didn't hoist yourself up the stairs to ask after my health."

DeKok, suddenly called back to reality, pulled an earlobe and laughed.

"That too, Kate. How are you?"

"Fine and you?"

"Getting on with it."

She pressed her lips together and nodded.

"Fine ... that's been dealt with," she said resolutely. "So, drop your pants."

DeKok grinned.

"Thanks anyway. I'm actually not here for that. You want to know why I'm here at, for you, an ungodly hour?"

"Exactly."

"Carol Ponytail."

"What do you want with her?"

"We need to chat."

"What about?"

DeKok hesitated for a moment.

"Jewelry," he said after a long pause.

Kate nodded slowly.

"Antique jewelry."

"How did you guess?"

Silly Kate did not answer. She picked up the magazine from her lap and heaved herself onto her feet. Her oversized slippers caused her to shuffle toward the window. In front of the window stood a table with a woolen tablecloth and a few chairs covered with the same material.

"Come," she said as she pulled out a few chairs. "I don't care to meet with you standing." She waited until the inspectors were seated. As she sat, she said, "I told Carol to watch it. I was sure you would come after her."

"You're talking about the jewels?"

Silly Kate nodded. She hoisted her heavy breasts up and rested them on the table as she leaned forward.

"Look, Carol has been going for years to old man

Vlaanderen at Gentleman's Canal. He treats her well. Really. No kinky stuff; no rough stuff. He never haggles and always gives her a generous personal tip. Carol genuinely likes him. Old man Vlaanderen is a gentleman, one of a dying breed. He understands that even a working girl is, before anything else, a human being. That's how he treats her."

DeKok resigned himself to let the praise for Vlaanderen wash over him. He had known Silly Kate for years and he knew she might shut up like a clam if you interrupted her discourse.

"Has ... has Carol ever seen the jewelry?" he tried carefully.

Silly Kate made a gesture of annoyance.

"I'm getting there," she said, testily. "Sometimes, when Carol is around, he takes the jewels out of the safe. With her clothes off, he adorns her. He dresses her hair with gold and silver combs. He adds a tiara, earrings, and a necklace so full of stones it covers her breasts. Next comes armbands, anklets, rings, jewel-studded belts ..." She closed her eyes and then looked silently into the distance. "Little Carol looks like a Christmas tree ... gorgeous ... everything glittering."

DeKok coughed discreetly.

"Have you ever told anyone else about these costume parties?"

Silly Kate shook her head indignantly.

"Never," she said. "We are professional women. I know when to keep my mouth shut."

"And Carol?"

Her face fell.

"You can warn a youngster, but sense comes with maturity." She patted her ample bosom. "I was the same way They don't call me *Silly Kate* for nothing. I used to spill my guts. A young pro relishes the power she has over Johns." She sighed. "Once life deals a few uppercuts, we learn prudence. But my name stuck."

DeKok understood.

"So, Carol *did* talk."

Silly Kate made a helpless gesture.

"Her best friend and confidante, Charlotte, hears it all. They don't keep any secrets from each other." She fell silent and brushed an invisible speck of dust from the tablecloth. "Charlotte is a wild woman, a married woman. She is always on the make. If a John wants a second girl, Carol never fails to invite Charlotte. She always goes along for the ride, not the money."

"She's not in the business?"

"No, she's in the theater."

"Really, what kind of theater?"

"Variety, carney, maybe the circus."

"Why do you say that?"

"She does a number with a knife thrower."

Vledder sank into the chair behind his desk. His face showed complete satisfaction. With a contented sigh he leaned back.

"It's coming together beautifully," he exclaimed happily. "Wonderful. We can close the case."

DeKok looked at him.

"Which case?"

The young inspector made a gesture of dismissal.

"Both cases," he said with a laugh. "Silly Kate just handed us the keys to the jewel theft and the murder."

DeKok pushed his lower lip out. It gave him a surprisingly disapproving face.

"Fine," he said finally, "then who is the culprit?"

"Fantinelli."

DeKok's mouth fell open in astonishment.

"Fantinelli?"

Vledder nodded with a self-satisfied smile on his lips.

"Remember the guy you didn't like for the murder? The guy who walked out of Warmoes on the strength of your intuition?"

DeKok listened to the sarcastic tone and grinned. The sarcasm did not bother him. He expected Vledder to voice his own opinions.

"And that *intuition,* hasn't changed," he said calmly.

Vledder leaned forward and pointed at the chair next to his desk.

"Why don't you sit down for a moment and I'll explain it all to you."

DeKok sat down on the indicated chair.

"I'm listening," he said patiently.

Vledder held up an index finger.

"It's really simple. The pattern of relationships sets the stage. Carol Ponytail, a. k. a Clarisse, can't resist blabbing to her girl, Charlotte. Her special "friend," Vlaanderen, decks her out in fabulous jewelry, blah, blah, blah. He gets stuff out of his safe, just to deck her out. No more discreet than Carol, Charlotte repeats the story to her knife-throwing husband."

"Good ... go on."

"Fantinelli maneuvers his wife into asking Carol to take a closer look at the combination to the safe, next time Vlaanderen indulges his taste for guilding her."

DeKok rubbed his chin.

"Okay, it could happen."

Vledder continued as if he had not heard his partner.

"As soon as Fantinelli gets the combination, he waits patiently for the next time Clarisse gets an invitation."

DeKok nodded agreement.

"Now we're to last weekend."

"Exactly. Clarisse, or whoever, makes sure Vlaanderen tuckers out and falls into a deep sleep. As soon as the old man is snoring, she gets up, borrows the key to the safe, lets Fantinelli in. He absconds with a fortune in jewelry." Vledder looked triumphant. "Cake, don't you think?"

DeKok rubbed his little finger along the bridge of his nose.

"And the death of the clown?"

Vledder gesticulated impatiently.

"A direct result of the burglary."

"How?"

"Charlotte."

DeKok looked puzzled.

"What about Charlotte?"

Vledder shook his head. It was so obvious.

"She was having an affair with the clown," he said impatiently. "She must have told Pierrot that her husband and best friend conspired to organize this easy, profitable burglary. When Pierrot hears about it, he demands part of the loot ... for himself and Charlotte. Fantinelli refuses, probably because he feels Pierrot is blackmailing him. The point is, he refuses. The two fight. Furious, Fantinelli grabs a throwing knife and kills the clown."

There was a long silence while DeKok stared thoughtfully in the distance. After a long pause DeKok spoke again.

"It *sounds* impressive," he said.

Vledder became agitated.

"It doesn't just *sound* impressive, it *is* impressive. My theory is undeniably solid. Fantinelli, himself, is so transparent."

"And you think you have the right stuff for an arrest?"

Vledder nodded with conviction.

"I was ready to roll this morning, before we knew the relationship between the two females."

DeKok nodded.

"I'm still trying to digest all the coincidences in the story you relate." He sighed, "Sadly, if your theory is correct, Silly Kate's Carol is guilty of criminal conspiracy. She is certainly an accessory to the burglary."

Vledder reacted angrily.

"Of course she's the driving force, worse than the others. It all revolves around her. Without her close cooperation, Fantinelli could never have pulled off the robbery. She has been Vlaanderen's companion for years. No doubt he trusted her. It's not hard to imagine Vlaanderen getting careless around her."

"You mean to say that it would be rather easy for Carol to get hold of the combination?"

"Exactly."

DeKok's phone rang. Out of habit, Vledder walked over and answered it. After a few seconds he covered the mouthpiece with his hands and shot DeKok a significant look.

"Carol Ponytail is downstairs," he said. "She wants to talk to you."

A boyish smile played around DeKok's lips.

"You're a lucky guy, Dick. You don't have to hunt down your perpetrators. They're offering themselves up on a silver platter."

Vledder saw DeKok's face and listened to the bantering undertone. He suddenly felt uneasy.

7

Carol Ponytail turned out to be delicious. She walked toward DeKok with a sensual sway of her hips, punctuated by the discrete clicking of her high-heeled shoes. She managed to look both elegant and provocative in a tight, short skirt of black velvet. Her silky white blouse showed precisely enough cleavage to entice.

The old inspector watched her with discreet approval. He was not immune to feminine beauty. With a friendly smile and a courteous bow he held a chair out for her next to his desk.

She seated herself with graceful poise and crossed her lovely legs. She glanced briefly at Vledder while she rearranged a strand of platinum hair. She spoke with the slightest Amsterdam accent.

"Mother sent me," she said.

DeKok nodded his understanding.

"I didn't know you called yourself Clarisse nowadays."

She shrugged her shoulders with a careless gesture that did exciting things to her cleavage.

"Carol is so common."

"Not for you."

"Hardly."

"Do you know why I asked you here?"

She nodded slowly.

"Vlaanderen's collection …" She suddenly changed her tone of voice and lifted her head. Her brown eyes sparkled. "Really, you don't have to lecture me. Mother already did that."

"With reason?"

"What do you mean?"

DeKok fiddled with a pencil in his hand.

"Have you talked with others about Vlaanderen's jewelry?"

"Just with Charlotte. Charlotte and I are very close. She confides in me, too."

"Tell me more."

"She said she was having a fling with the dead clown. She said Fantinelli was enraged by this affair. He threw her make-up table around the dressing room and called her a bitch in heat."

"Nasty."

Carol shook her head.

"Sure, but who could judge him? Charlotte will bed any guy she meets. Some of us do it for the money and derive no pleasure out of it … not much, anyway."

DeKok kept a neutral expression.

"But Charlotte always enjoys it?"

Carol nodded with a sly smile on her face.

"You could say that."

"How long have you known Charlotte?"

"A little over two years."

"So, you must have heard a lot about her various affairs."

Carol tittered.

"Charlotte gets very excited with each new conquest. She enjoys making a man dance to her tune."

"It is easy to see how Fantinelli would be fed up over yet another affair," DeKok said pensively.

"Yes."

"Even so, she continues to perform in the knife act."

Carol's face showed a pretty frown.

"You mean, she's not afraid he'll miss one of these days?"

"Exactly."

A patronizing smile played around her lips.

"You don't know how most knife-throwing acts operate."

"Tell me."

"Sure the knife thrower throws *some* knives, but for really dangerous stunts, he doesn't throw any at all. He makes the knife disappear when he throws, something like a magician does. Then the knife appears in the target, triggered from behind. When Charlotte is on the wheel, for instance, she's perfectly safe."

"I did not known that. It seems Charlotte is never in real danger."

"Not from Fantinelli. Fantinelli needs Charlotte. Aside from the act, they have a deep, intense relationship. Fantinelli is obsessed with her, you know what I mean?"

"I think I understand," DeKok said carefully. He leaned forward. "Does Charlotte also share all her secrets with her husband?"

Carol grinned mischievously.

"I don't think so."

"I mean your secrets. Did she tell him about the jewelry?"

Carol's face froze.

"You don't mean," she said, hesitating, "you aren't suggesting Fantinelli stole the jewels."

DeKok made a nonchalant gesture.

"I'm just exploring the possibilities."

Decisively, Carol shook her head.

"Fantinelli is no jewel thief, definitely not. He's not capable." She spread her hands, "Fantinelli is like a hapless, grown-up child. He's a kid, whose father happened to teach him how to throw knives." She paused. "Were it not for Charlotte he couldn't even do that."

DeKok heard the tone of disdain.

"Is Charlotte such a strong personality or is she manipulative?"

"She has him mesmerized, ready to do her bidding."

"And what about you?"

"What?"

"Does she have your number, as well?"

Carol's gaze drifted away. She remained silent while she mulled over the question.

"Sometimes," she said after a long pause, "she tries being in control." It sounded vague. "Sometimes she would like me to bend to her will."

"And?"

"No worries," she said firmly. "She'll never succeed. You see, I am a *woman.*"

"You mean her domination works only on men?"

She nodded a few times.

"Yes," she said slowly, "you got it." Suddenly she lifted her head. DeKok saw raw fear in her eyes. "Pierrot, oh my god," she blurted.

"What about Pierrot?"

Carol swallowed nervously.

"Pierrot, Pieter. She told *him* about the jewelry."

DeKok gave Vledder a mocking look.

"What, no arrest? Did you not see me look at you before I told her she could leave? Your mouth never moved. You looked like a deer in headlights." He waved in the direction of the door. "It was her, wasn't it, you accused of being at the center of it all? How did it go? Oh, yes, I remember. 'It all revolves around her. Without her cooperation, Fantinelli could never have pulled off the robbery.'"

Vledder hung his head.

"I didn't dare detain her," he said with a sigh. "It took only a few minutes to convince me Carol wasn't involved."

DeKok grinned.

"Were you acting on fact or feeling?"

Vledder turned away. He had trouble looking his colleague in the eye.

"Feeling," he admitted weakly.

DeKok smiled.

"You'll be a good cop, one day," he said. It was sincere. "Never underestimate feelings. Go with your gut instinct."

With a sad face, Vledder shook his head.

"I couldn't bring myself to ask if there was some way she could have obtained the combination of the safe." He glanced at DeKok. "I noticed you didn't ask, either."

"Do you think it was necessary?"

Vledder shrugged his shoulders. He was regaining his composure.

"Until an hour ago, I liked her for conspiracy. If anybody was in a position to get the combination she was." The young inspector spread his hands in a helpless gesture. "Who does that leave? Maurice, the son?" He snorted. "Or maybe we could look into the supernatural ... gremlins, for instance, or, eh, the pinch horrors."

"The what?" asked DeKok.

"The pinch horrors," laughed Vledder. "It's an invention of Inspector Vries. Whenever he's faced with an inexplicable theft, he uses that as an excuse."

DeKok shook his head. He looked serious.

"We must keep one thing in mind. The theft from Vlaanderen is not isolated. It's one of a string of similar burglaries, all very cleverly concocted. We do not have a plague of gremlins, or a rash of *pinch horrors*. That is a fact and I think there is a real brain behind it all."

"Who?"

DeKok gave him a tired smile.

"Good question," he nodded. "But speculation would be premature. Certainly we cannot construct a sensible answer right now." He lifted his head and stuck out his chin. His face changed into a steel mask. "It's a shot in the dark," he said grimly, "but I promise an answer in the very near future."

Vledder looked at him with a frown.

"The notion persists whether Pierrot's murder is connected to the thefts. Charlotte couldn't help admitting he knew about Vlaanderen's jewelry collection." He thought for a moment. "Perhaps that knowledge proved fatal."

DeKok was all unfeigned admiration.

"Dick," he said, "you sometimes say very intelligent things."

Vledder almost blushed.

"What about Charlotte?" he asked.

DeKok grinned.

"She's arrestingly beautifully and, apparently, a very sensual woman. She enjoys flitting from one man to the next." He gazed into the distance, momentarily preoccupied.

Suddenly he resumed, "Flit ... flutter. What insect flits from flower to flower?"

"A bee?"

"No, no, it's a—"

Vledder interrupted.

"A butterfly."

DeKok nodded.

"Butterfly," he repeated, yes indeed. Suddenly he vaulted to grab his coat and hat.

Vledder followed.

"Where are we going?"

The gray sleuth turned toward his young friend as he struggled into his coat.

"We're going to pay another visit to Dongen, perhaps he can tell us where we can recruit a butterfly."

Peter Dongen, the tall impresario, received the inspectors politely. With a friendly gesture he invited them to follow him to his cluttered office.

"Have you identified the false Pierrot?" he asked. "The next morning, after the unsettling experience at the morgue, I called Groningen a second time. Nobody there could give me any further details. The performance of the fake Pierrot was flawless. Nobody imagined he could be an impostor."

DeKok looked surprised. Again he was struck by the warm, melodious tone of Dongen's voice.

"I regret to inform you," he said, a bit sheepishly, "that we have not yet started an investigation in that direction."

It was Dongen's turn to be surprised.

"Aren't you interested in the fake Pierrot?"

DeKok nodded.

"He has my attention, I assure you. The fake Pierrot is central to our investigation. He's certainly a person of interest."

"What is your interest?"

DeKok smiled politely.

"The imposter knew the real Pierrot would not appear. In other words, he probably knew the real Pierrot had been killed. He would have known long before we discovered the body." He waved a hand in the air. "That puts him in close proximity to the murder or the murderer."

Dongen invited them to sit down.

"So you think the fake Pierrot committed the murder?" he asked after they were seated.

DeKok placed his little hat on the floor.

"It's, eh, it's one possibility," he said carefully. "But it isn't the only one. Someone else could have sent him to perform in Pierrot's stead. When we recovered the body, the man had been dead for at least six hours. Death would have occurred around three o'clock in the afternoon. No matter how our pretend Pierrot gained the knowledge, he had plenty of time to prepare." DeKok sighed and rubbed the back of his neck. "Frankly," he added, "I'm a bit bothered by the false Pierrot."

"How?"

DeKok grimaced.

"Why did he appear as Pierrot, there in Groningen, knowing the real Pierrot was dead?"

Dongen did not answer at once. He crossed his legs, leaned back in his chair, and placed the tips of his fingers together.

"That seems rather obvious to me," he said finally. "He was providing himself or the actual perpetrator an alibi."

"But did he?"

The impresario grinned self-consciously.

"I'm just an amateur, inspector. But the idea of an alibi seems obvious. You see, the clown is dead … the clown performs."

DeKok gave the impresario a long, searching look.

"But does a corpse need an alibi?"

Peter Dongen shook his head.

"The corpse, of course not. But the killer …"

DeKok nodded encouragingly.

"Now I see where you're going. The murderer would benefit from an alibi. My problem is the performance in Groningen. It only serves to put us on the track of 'Clown Number 2' … and from him, to the killer."

"But can you find him?"

DeKok pushed his lower lip forward.

"Not easily. As somebody put it yesterday: 'What is a clown? A clown is nothing … absolutely nothing—a crazy costume, big shoes, and a snoot full of paint.'" Effortlessly, DeKok repeated Fantinelli's statement.

Dongen laughed.

"I never quite thought of it that way, but it makes sense."

DeKok stood up.

"I would like a list of the artists who performed on the same bill with Pierrot on the night in question, in Groningen." He paused. "And I want the address of Butterfly."

Dongen gave him a puzzled look.

"Butterfly?"

DeKok nodded.

The impresario laughed nervously.

"You're the second person to ask me that."

DeKok's eyebrows suddenly performed peculiar gymnastics as Dongen sifted through piles on his desk.

"Who was the first one to ask?"

Peter Dongen was still searching and did not look up when he answered.

"Maurice ... Maurice Vlaanderen," he said.

8

From Dongen's office at Willem Park Way, DeKok and Vledder drove in the direction of Baerle Street. Despite the proximity of the two streets, they could not make the turn directly onto Baerle Street. They diverted, going around the Van Gogh Museum and the Concert Gebouw. Traffic was murder. Brown-painted steel poles, decorated with the shield of Amsterdam, had been placed along all major streets to prevent parking on the sidewalks and help guide traffic. These "Amsterdammmertjes" (Little Amsterdammers) had the opposite effect.

Unable to park on the sidewalks, people simply started parking and double-parking in the roadway. Amsterdam's narrow streets could not absorb this congestion. Tricky traffic patterns had turned to complete chaos. Vledder managed to make progress by total disregard for the traffic laws and by completely ignoring the disapproving honking of other cars. Most other drivers took one look at the battered VW and decided that the driver would not mind a collision.

DeKok grumbled that they could have walked the distance in a fraction of the time. But after a while he sank back in his seat and concentrated on the case.

Little Lowee had told him there was a performer known as Butterfly connected to the same group as the murdered clown. Since that time he felt as if part of his burden had been lifted. Combining his investigation of the theft with that of the murder gave him a renewed sense of purpose. Although he wasn't certain both cases were related, the diminutive barkeeper had given him a weapon in his argument with the commissaris. Now he would be justified in his refusal to concentrate just on the burglaries.

He grinned to himself. He could predict the commissaris, prompted by the judge advocate, would nag him again about the burglaries. He silently enjoyed the prospect of the next interview with his chief. The outcome would be in his favor.

When the police car completed its detour they found themselves in a quieter neighborhood. Vledder looked aside. There was a question he simply had to ask.

"What does Maurice want with Butterfly?"

DeKok pushed back his little hat and hoisted himself up in the seat.

"Perhaps he, too, has discovered the dancer called Butterfly. Like us, maybe he'd like to know whether she is connected to the robbery."

"But how could he have enough to connect the dots?"

DeKok shrugged.

"We'll have to ask him." He paused, then added, "Apparently Maurice didn't know so much. That's why he visited Dongen."

"Do you think he beat us to her?"

DeKok grunted.

"He could have, or he could be en route. He's known her address a few hours longer." He looked around. "Are we going the right way? You seem to be wandering in and out of three different neighborhoods."

"Blame it on the traffic. Anyway we're almost there.

There's Patrick Henry Street." Vledder took a wrinkled piece of paper out of his breast pocket. "Number 764 … I think it's just past that little park there."

DeKok lifted his ridiculous little hat and bowed formally.

"My name is DeKok … with a kay-oh-kay. I'm an inspector assigned to Warmoes Street Station." He thumbed in the direction of Vledder. "And this is my colleague, Detective Vledder."

With the door in her hand she looked suspiciously at the two men.

"Police?"

DeKok nodded.

"And you? You are Butterfly?"

A faint smile curled her lips.

"That's what my colleagues call me."

"People in the theater group?"

"Yes."

DeKok shaped his face into a friendly, winning expression.

"We would like to talk with you."

"What about?"

"The death of a clown."

She looked frightened.

"That … that is—"

DeKok interrupted gently.

"Maybe we should step inside. This doesn't seem a subject to discuss on the doorstep."

She blushed. She opened the door wider and indicated that the inspectors should come ahead. She stretched out her left arm.

"First door on the right. Find yourselves a seat."

It sounded friendly and inviting. Carefully she closed and latched the door. Then she followed them.

Vledder and DeKok found seats on a wide, leather sofa with broad armrests. Butterfly pushed a hassock closer. She settled herself in a languid pose, but she had the sinewy strength of a dancer. With a quick, almost prim gesture she folded the slips of her dressing gown over her knees.

"I must tell you I know nothing about the death of that man."

Before answering DeKok gave her his policeman's gaze, sustained and searching. Without coyness his gaze felt her features. Little Lowee, he thought, was right. Butterfly was an enticing beauty. The diminutive barkeep, frequently surrounded by prostitutes, had a discerning eye for quality. She was beautiful, slender, and, on the surface, fragile. Her small oval face had charm. Although DeKok estimated her to be in her late twenties, her figure was that of a sixteen-year-old girl.

"Did you know Pierrot well?" he began.

She pursed her lips.

"We were acquainted, not intimately. But we all treated each other cordially."

"Who?"

"The members of our group. It was always very friendly, more like family. As in any family, there were some clashes ... differences of opinion." She smiled shyly. "Artists can be temperamental."

DeKok nodded encouragingly.

"You speak in the past tense. Has the group disbanded?"

She shook her head. Her lovely, shy smile faded into an expression of sadness.

"Ever since we declared bankruptcy, we've had to stop

performing as a group. It's a pity. We seldom see one another. Everyone is now on his, or her, own trying to get gigs. It's not always easy. One misses the support … especially me. All alone I'm not that much of an attraction."

DeKok leaned forward.

"Do you know a Mr. Vlaanderen?"

Butterfly suddenly sat up straight and pressed her lips together. She gave DeKok an accusing look.

"This morning," she said after a brief pause, "I got a phone call from a Mr. Vlaanderen." Her voice rose and her face reddened. "He was ill-mannered, boorish. He told me that I had to return the jewels immediately."

DeKok feigned surprise.

"What jewels?"

She gestured with both hands.

"Search me. This Vlaanderen gave me one chance to come clean and avoid going to prison. If I returned the jewels today, he would keep the police out of it."

"And?"

"What?"

"Are you returning them?"

Angrily she stood up and stamped a dainty foot on the floor.

"Listen—I have no jewels," she screamed loudly. "Before he called to threaten me, I'd never heard of a Vlaanderen."

DeKok's face showed no emotion. But he noticed that her angrily contorted face lost none of its beauty.

"Please sit down," he said softly, but it sounded like a command.

Pouting, she sank down on the hassock. She took a small, lace handkerchief from her pocket and delicately dabbed at her eyes.

"What on earth does he want from me?" She lowered her head and sobbed quietly. "I have no jewels ... none that belong to anyone else!"

"What about yourself?"

She sobbed again.

"Onyx," she said. "I have some onyx jewelry. I like onyx."

DeKok picked up his hat from the floor and stood up.

"Just one more question, who is to blame for you and your colleagues going broke?"

She lifted a teary face up to him.

"Pierrot ... he took off with our money."

They got into their car and drove away from Patrick Henry Street. Vledder made a turn toward Nassau Canal. He shook his head.

"What a child-woman," he sighed. "Weren't you tempted to take her under your arm? I'd put her in a gilded cage to protect her from this harsh world."

DeKok looked at his young colleague and laughed.

"You're waxing romantic," he said with some amazement. "I've never heard you like that before."

"Well," shrugged Vledder, "she was so helpless, just a slip of a girl. You were much too harsh. I felt downright sorry for her."

DeKok grinned unrepentantly.

"That helplessness could very well be an act, a diversion. Perhaps our little Butterfly is not at all as vulnerable as she appears. Showbiz is a hard profession ... a dog-eat-dog world."

"You mean she would not have lasted this long if she weren't made of steel?"

"That's precisely what I mean."

Vledder shifted into a lower gear and suddenly hit the accelerator to push the underpowered VW across a rather steep bridge.

"You think," he said as they coasted down the other side of the bridge, "she could have something to do with the burglaries?"

DeKok thought about it, as he mulled over the conversation. He remembered her various expressions.

"I think," he said after a while, "it may be a good idea to get some more background information on her." He glanced at his partner. "Did you note her real name?"

"Sure I did … and you remember it as well. It's Martha—Martha Hagen."

DeKok nodded.

"That's right. Why don't you find out if she's married or ever has been. Has she had steady, or less than steady, relationships with men or women? What schooling … that sort of thing."

"But," protested Vledder, "why didn't you ask her when you had the chance?"

"Didn't think of it," answered DeKok carelessly. "Besides," he added, "we would have had to check it out anyway."

Vledder looked disgruntled.

"More work for me, but all right." He changed his tone of voice. "Are we going to do anything about that bankruptcy?"

"Pierrot's absconding with the money?"

"Yes. Don't you find that intriguing?"

DeKok looked suddenly aggressive.

"Indeed," he agreed grimly. "Suddenly all the members of that Variety Group are suspects in the murder." He turned in his seat. "Remember what she said about artists being temperamental ... it's just another way to say irritable and unpredictable." He sighed. "Think about it. It's a wonder Pierrot lived as long as he did."

They left the car about a block from the station house, walking the rest of the way. As they got inside, the watch commander notified them a man was waiting for them.

"Kuster looked down his nose a bit. He's been waiting for more than an hour," he said disapprovingly.

DeKok looked at the large clock over the desk. It was fifteen minutes past six o'clock.

"Vledder and I," he said, a bit irked, "have been working all day. We wouldn't mind a bite to eat first."

Kuster quickly interrupted.

"You can't do that. First talk to the man."

DeKok rubbed the corner of his eyes with a tired gesture.

"All right, who is he?"

"He says he's a friend."

"Whose friend?"

"Pieter Eikelbos' friend."

DeKok managed a tired grin and climbed the stairs to the detective room. Vledder detoured to fetch the visitor from the waiting room. DeKok awaited the two in the upstairs corridor. As Vledder and the visitor approached DeKok, the man reached out to shake hands.

"You're Inspector DeKok?"

"With a kay-oh-kay," admitted DeKok as he shook hands.

The man smiled for a moment.

"The watch commander told me you'd say so."

Without comment DeKok led their visitor into the detective room and offered him a chair next to his desk. He tossed his raincoat and hat at the peg, missing both shots. He sat down behind his desk.

"You're a friend of Pierrot?" he asked curtly.

The man shook his head.

"I'm a friend of *Pieter Eikelbos.*" He emphasized the name.

DeKok looked surprised.

"Is there a difference?"

The man nodded with conviction.

"For anyone who knew him, yes, because Pierrot was nothing but a mask. The clown disguise hid Pieter's true nature. In fact, Pieter hated Pierrot. But it was the only way he could be invisible, while on stage."

"Invisible?"

The man cocked his head.

"This won't be difficult for you. You're a police inspector. An understanding of human nature goes with the territory." He paused. "So this isn't farfetched."

DeKok nodded and observed the wrinkly face of the man. Suddenly, without reason, he felt empathy for his visitor.

"Let's start with your name," he said.

"As I said ... a friend."

DeKok shook his head.

"You will have to do better. What is your name?"

"Jonkers, Henri Jonkers. I live in the Jordaan, on Daisy Street ... Number 317."

DeKok nodded. The *Jordaan* was one of the oldest neighborhoods in Amsterdam. The name was a bastardization of the French word *Jardin,* garden. It was so called by the

Huguenots, who sought refuge in the Netherlands. They fled religious persecution in France. All the streets in the "garden" had flower names.

"How long have you known Pieter?"

"Ages. I witnessed his birth, so to speak. I was ... eh, a family friend of his parents."

"Where you close?"

"We were together from an early age. Once we were grown I still visited him in his houseboat. We would catch up with each other and he would end up talking about his troubles."

"He had a troubled life?"

Jonkers nodded to himself.

"Yes, he had a weakness ... an addiction."

"Drugs?"

"No, it wasn't drugs—nor women, despite what you may have heard. Women offered themselves to him, you know. Some were just curious about the man behind the costume. But he never was the instigator."

"So, what, exactly was his addiction?"

"He was a compulsive gambler."

"He gambled?" asked DeKok. "Is that why he took the money?"

Jonkers sighed deeply.

"Pieter believed his luck would change. Then he would be able to pay back all the money he owed with interest. That's why he always played *va banque.*"

DeKok nodded.

"*Va banque,* double or nothing, but it always came up nothing."

Jonkers looked the inspector in the eye.

"His luck ran out, so I want to give you the name of his murderer."

DeKok gaped in disbelief.

"His murderer?"

Henri Jonkers stared at DeKok without emotion.

"Freddie," he said, "Freddie Wezel."

9

After a long, refreshing night's sleep, DeKok's mind had been revived after the previous day's exhaustive nature. He whistled cheerily, but tunelessly, as he entered the crowded detective room. With a casual gesture he threw his lunch bag in a drawer. Only then did he glance at Vledder who was busy on his computer.

"What are you doing?" he asked by way of greeting.

Vledder's flying fingers rested for a moment.

"I'm just organizing everything we know, so far. I'm also preparing a report of our activities. All we have, though, is a hotchpotch of unrelated facts. Nothing parallels anything else."

"Oh, well," DeKok said after a long pause. "I'm sure you'll be able to arrange it in an acceptable form."

Vledder grinned ruefully.

"I better," he said. "Buitendam has asked for you."

"What does he want? More reports?"

Vledder shrugged.

"He doesn't talk much to me. He just said he wanted to see you."

DeKok's face became stony.

"He'll have to wait," DeKok muttered, already sounding annoyed.

He closed the drawer of his desk and began pacing up

and down the crowded room. He managed to unconsciously avoid obstacles like carelessly placed chairs and dustbins. He sidestepped the moving chairs of his colleagues as they rolled from one desk to another.

It was one of his habits to walk off difficult problems. His thoughts formed more clearly during this slow, deliberate pacing. The latest turn in the convoluted clown case caught him off-guard. It took him into uncharted territory. Suddenly he stopped next to Vledder's desk.

"A rat," he said with disgust. It sounded like the conclusion of a long analysis.

Vledder looked up.

"What?"

"Freddie Wezel."

"You know him?"

DeKok nodded with a grimace on his face.

"Oh, yes. He's been holed up in the quarter for some twenty years now. In the old days they called him *Lady Freddie*. He conned the public with three-card-monte. You know, three cards and you're supposed to guess where the Lady is, after he shuffles them around."

Vledder laughed.

"And the suckers always get it wrong."

"No, not at first. As I said, he's a rat. To gain their trust, he would let his victims win, at first. Two out of three hands would be a winner. As the stakes grew higher and higher, he'd shut them down. Next he set up some back rooms. At first these were in abandoned buildings, sort of like floating crap games. Later he took over houses of people who owed him money. Gambling in houses lent his scams some respectability, you see. An unwilling host would invite guests to a party. Freddie would be on hand to skin the guests, mostly the host's close friends. Then he moved on, establishing an actual casino in a house along St. Nicholas Street. The police finally forced him out by raiding the place constantly. Regardless of the pretext for a raid, they always found something. If he wasn't serving minors, he was watering drinks. He violated fire codes, got behind in his taxes. The beat goes on and on."

Vledder looked thoughtful.

"Even so, is he capable of murder?"

DeKok rubbed his chin in thought.

"He's managed to stay under the major crime radar," he said carefully. "Freddie is sly and sneaky ... the slippery type. We have a few unsolved murders among the closed case files. I'm personally convinced he had a hand in some or all of them. I simply reviewed those cases, out of my jurisdiction, you see. We've know he threatened and, maybe, strong-armed people who owed him money."

"Like Pierrot?"

DeKok sank down in the chair behind his desk.

"Pieter Eikelbos confessed as much to Henri Jonkers. He told his friend that Freddie Wezel had threatened him. There is no reason to doubt Jonkers. His story casts a new light on Pierrot's actions. He misused theater group funds, perhaps out of panic. They subsequently went belly-up. Question is, did Freddie's threats end in murder? It looks as though Pierrot's lifeline was cut the day the group filed bankruptcy."

Vledder nodded and made a few changes in the text on his computer screen. He read over what he had just entered.

"While Pieter Eikelbos remained in charge of the group's finances, he had a financial cushion. As soon as the money ran out, he couldn't pay his gambling debts. Coincidentally he wound up dead."

"And that—" began DeKok.

"Brings us right back to Freddie Wezel," completed Vledder.

"That's about it," agreed DeKok. He looked stern. "My worry is we'll never be able to prove it." He pointed out the window. "This is reminiscent of some cases gathering dust at headquarters."

"Identical?"

"More or less."

Vledder jumped up. His face had turned red.

"This is too much for me," he exclaimed. "We do not permit people to get away with murder in the Netherlands!" He spread his arms in bewilderment. "There *has* to be a way to hang this creep."

DeKok looked at his young colleague with a sad smile on his lips.

"You know what else?" he asked.

"What?"

"I know where Freddie opened his new gambling joint."

"Where?"

"On Gelder Quay, not far from Criers' Tower where we found the corpse."

Commissaris Buitendam greeted DeKok amiably. He even managed a stiff bow before he reseated himself.

"I'm glad, DeKok," he said in a friendly tone of voice, "you could find the time to visit with me. I have come to realize the investigation of the disappearing jewelry is consuming your time and effort. I sympathize." He paused and waved a slender, elegant hand at a stack of files on his desk.

The pile was almost a foot high. The commissaris face was animated. "They have arrived," he said happily.

"What?" DeKok asked the question in a suspicious tone.

The smile disappeared from the commissarial face and changed to a puzzled look.

"The files from The Hague," he said anxiously. "Our own judge advocate, Mr. Schaap, personally requested them. He wants you to have the complete picture. Therefore I advise you to study the dossiers carefully."

DeKok pointed at the stack of paper with a mocking grin.

"That pile of nonsense?" There was contempt in his voice.

The veins in Buitendam's neck corded. A vein popped out on his forehead. He placed his hands on the dossiers.

"This is not nonsense," he said, his voice barely under control. "These are bona fide reports, prepared by professional investigators."

DeKok looked at the stack and shook his head.

"I don't intend to read a single letter," he said stubbornly. "Let The Hague clean its own house."

Commissaris Buitendam stood up.

"Mr. Schaap has committed his resources to the Department of Justice in The Hague." He slapped the pile of documents with a flat hand. "You *will* include these reports in your investigation."

DeKok crossed his arms and then used one hand to rub his chin. He looked pensive. He did not really dislike his chief. That said, he had an irresistible urge to get the man's goat, whenever they were in close proximity. It was like prodding a blowfish to see it puff up. Dangerous, yes, but

DeKok couldn't keep himself from taking a poke. For his part, Buitendam rarely disappointed.

"Well, you keep them safe," he said after a long pause. "When I get around to it, I'll keep it in mind. For the time being … for now, I don't have any time for it."

Buitendam swallowed.

"No time … no time," he stammered.

DeKok made a helpless gesture.

"We've discussed this … it is *my* priority."

The commissaris' face puffed, turning purple. The vein throbbed. His eyes bulged.

"I forbid you DeKok, you are off the murder case."

The gray sleuth slowly shook his head.

"If you wish," he said solemnly. "However, those society burglaries may never be solved."

For a moment it looked like Buitendam was going to reach across his desk and take DeKok by the throat. Then he sighed deeply and stretched out a commanding arm toward the door.

"OUT!!"

DeKok left.

Vledder looked concerned.

"Have you been thrown out … again?"

DeKok nodded calmly, outwardly unruffled.

"The man is stupid," he said tiredly. Then he corrected himself. "It isn't that. He simply doesn't get it. He should just have asked me where we were in our investigations. Then I could have told him about the bankruptcy, the theater group, and a dancer by the name of Butterfly." He grinned without amusement. "Now he ordered me not to have anything further to do with the murder case."

"And you're going to let it go?"

DeKok shook his head.

"Not now that I have a Butterfly."

Vledder gave him a long, pensive look.

"So, you're telling me Martha Hagen did the burglaries?"

"Well," shrugged DeKok, "she's the only Butterfly we've found so far."

Vledder shook his head in resignation.

"You're on the wrong trail, DeKok," he said reasonably. "I've come to realize there is no connection between Pierrot's murder and the burglaries. Even so I empathize with your disinterest in the jewelry thefts. We would both rather concentrate on the murder first." He shook his head and smiled. "Our little Butterfly doesn't factor into the equation."

DeKok observed his young colleague with a measured look.

"That woman made some impression on you."

"Yes," nodded Vledder. "She has a sweet, warm personality. To see her as a criminal is ... eh, is ... twisted."

DeKok allowed the lines around his mouth to flicker. It was not a real laugh, not a sign of happiness, but a mild expression of self-mockery.

"I have suffered from a morbid imagination for years. Twisted or not, I use it to fight morbid crime." He sighed deeply. "We don't have the luxury of being fooled by a sweet face and charming manners," he chastised. Suddenly he narrowed his eyes as he looked at Vledder. "Where did you get the 'sweet, warm personality' part?"

Vledder looked apologetic.

"Well, you told me to get more detail."

"Yes, and so what?"

"Just so you know, I looked at her file. Martha Hagen has no rap sheet. We have nothing, not even a traffic ticket. I also called Dongen, her impresario."

"So he was the one who described her as sweet and warm?"

Vledder hesitated.

"Yes, and he went on to say Martha Hagen was the soul of that group of artists. It wasn't her performance on stage, but her poise and congeniality. She was the glue—she arbitrated differences, acted as a messenger between lovers. It all revolved around her."

DeKok nodded thoughtfully.

"And Dongen also called her Butterfly?"

"Yes," laughed Vledder. "It's her stage name. Nobody ever called her Martha Hagen. Peter Dongen knew her real name because of the contracts he arranged. People in the group called her Butterfly, or sometimes Ma."

"Ma?"

"Short for *Madame Butterfly,* the opera, you see."

"All that stemming from a dance number with a couple of plastic wings and a cable?" There was disbelief in his voice.

Vledder sighed.

"According to Dongen she had only the one number."

"Affairs, relationships?"

Vledder shrugged.

"Dongen couldn't say. He had never personally noticed anything."

"What about her past?"

"He was vague. The word among the group was she had studied the violin at the Conservatory as a youngster."

"Violin?"

Vledder nodded.

"Of course it's unverified. I'll check it out as soon as I have an opportunity. According to what she told people, she couldn't make any money with her violin. Therefore she changed to dance lessons. She landed a membership in the group more or less by accident."

"Who introduced her?"

Vledder looked up.

"Fantinelli."

10

Vledder and DeKok walked from the station house to Gelder Quay. It was unusually quiet in the narrow alleys of the inner city. On the corner of the sea dike, there was a small group of drug dealers. They chattered in rapid, wildly difficult Bargoens. There was an uncomfortable silence as the two inspectors passed the group. DeKok was a recognizable figure. They resumed their conversations once the two inspectors were out of earshot. In the houses along the narrow side of Gelder Quay, prostitutes were slowly getting geared up.

DeKok asked Vledder the time. It was almost eleven o'clock. DeKok hoped that Freddie would be having his breakfast about now. He knew Freddie's habits well enough. The gambler seldom rose before noon.

They stopped beside The Criers' Tower and looked through the iron fence at the small dock beneath the tower. Nearly three days had passed since the discovery of Picrrot's body. The investigation was going nowhere fast. The murderer and his motive were still hidden somewhere in the maze.

DeKok stared at the water. In his mind's eye he calculated the waterways that led to the tower. During construction of the Metro, access to the tower was limited for months. Now everything was open again. The waters in this vicinity could be reached by boat from almost anywhere. East of The Criers' Tower one could proceed through Easter Dock directly to Ijssel Lake and, from there, to the Zuyder Zee. To the west the waterways opened up into an extensive canal system running through the city. From there one could proceed inland in any direction and to the North Sea. There were no traces of anything in the water. Before moving on he took a last look at the dock. A few used condoms floated nearby. Some lazy prostitute had emptied the dustbin from her room into the canal.

They walked around The Criers' Tower to Prince Henry's Quay. They entered the wider part of Gelder Quay. DeKok stopped in front of a heavy oaken door with a barred hatch at eye height. DeKok leaned on the bell knob on the side of the door. One minute seemed like ten. As the hatch opened they saw part of a man's face behind the bars. DeKok recognized one of the bouncers of the gambling den and gave him a friendly grin.

"Do you know me?"

"DeKok," growled the man. "Warmoes Street."

"Very good," said DeKok and lifted his hat a centimeter in the air. "Open up. We're here to see Freddie."

The man made a movement with his head.

"Freddie's still asleep."

"Then you wake him."

The man hesitated.

"What's this all about?"

DeKok wiped the grin off his face.

"Murder," he said evenly.

The man grimaced as if he had heard a dirty word.

"Murder?" he repeated, not quite believing his ears.

"Murder," confirmed DeKok. "Tell Freddie we will not move from in front of this door until I have spoken to him."

The man closed the hatch and DeKok glanced at his watch. More than five minutes later the door opened. The same man preceded the inspectors down a long, marble corridor. At the end of the corridor a carved wooden staircase rose in a half circle to the second floor. The man pushed a switch next to a leather-covered doorknob. The door sprang open. The man looked at DeKok with a smile.

"We've just updated our security," he said pleasantly. "If I throw a switch downstairs, not even a mouse can get in, or out."

DeKok looked at him.

"You found that necessary, did you?"

DeKok knew there was a constant state of war between the various underground gambling dens. Most bosses paid thugs to break up competitive establishments. The resulting collateral damage was never reported to the police. Victims waited until the time was right and exacted their revenge in kind.

Without answering DeKok's question, the man took the inspectors to a large room furnished with about a dozen comfortable club chairs.

"Please take a seat … Freddie is dressing."

Soon a stocky man emerged from a side door. He had a rough face, jowls like dewlaps, and a nose crooked from being broken various times. His thin, flaxen hair was combed over and plastered down. He wore a purple dressing gown. A polka-dot Ascot covered his neck.

He approached DeKok with long strides. They shook hands. He ignored Vledder. He pulled up a club chair and sat down opposite the inspectors. He lit a cigarette and leaned back. After he had blown a smoke ring at the ceiling, he lowered his gaze.

"Murder, DeKok?" he asked mockingly.

DeKok grinned.

"What do you call sliding six inches of steel into somebody's back?"

Freddie Wezel tapped his chest.

"I'm supposed to have done that?"

DeKok pointed at the high windows.

"Very near here, on the other side of the water, on the dock at the foot of Criers' Tower we found the corpse of a dead Pierrot. A little birdie told me he owed you a lot of money." DeKok's smile was fixed. "What made me think of you is your very persuasive collection methods." He did not finish, but leaned forward.

"Freddie, did this Pierrot owe you money?"

"A gambling debt is a debt of honor."

DeKok shook his head.

"You're not answering my question. Did he owe you money?"

"Yes."

"How much?"

"That's none of your business."

DeKok smiled.

"I understand—enough to compel you to apply a little pressure." It sounded just a little too friendly.

Freddie made an irritated gesture.

"When they win, they expect me to cough up the cash."

DeKok ignored the remark.

"Did you threaten Pierrot?"

Freddie took a long pull on his cigarette and slowly released the smoke.

"Look here, DeKok," he said patiently, "I don't want

to hear the word *threat* again. As I said, a gambling debt
is a debt of honor. Every gambler knows that. The people
who come here regularly get credit, as much as they need.
Pierrot was one of my regulars." He slapped the armrest of
his chair. "If one of these associates doesn't pay up on time,
I'm not going to beg ... but I *will* remind them of their
obligations."

"Like Pierrot?"

Freddie nodded calmly.

"Like Pierrot," he said.

"And that's why you went to his house?"

"Yes, his payment was more than a week late and he
didn't show. That's like a red flag to me, a warning sign.
Therefore I paid him a visit in his houseboat."

"Just you?"

Freddie grinned.

"I don't need any witnesses."

"When were you on that houseboat?"

The gambler closed his eyes for a moment. Then he
opened them again.

"Three days," he said, "three days before his death."

DeKok leaned his head to one side.

"When was his time up?"

"You mean the deadline for payment?"

"Exactly."

For the first time Wezel showed some emotion.

"The night he turned up dead," he said hoarsely.

DeKok's expression remained fixed.

"Remarkable coincidence, don't you think?"

Freddie hoisted himself upright in his chair.

"The hell with coincidence," he spoke louder. "I had
nothing to do with offing the loser." He tapped his forehead

with an index finger. "I'm not a mental case. You think if I whack a guy I'm going to do him on my own doorstep?"

DeKok ignored the question.

"Was it the first time he was late with a payment?

Freddie Wezel again sank back in his chair. He shook his head, as if to clear it.

"No, things weren't going well for Pierrot. Something smelled. He bet heavily, kept losing. He needed more and more credit, but the payments became fewer. For a while I took it easy on him. I gave him a couple of friendly warnings, even suggested he stop gambling for a while, until he paid down his debt. Nobody starts with the heavy stuff right away."

"But eventually you had no choice, eh? The situation got heavy, I guess."

The gambler sighed.

"He gave me no choice. At the end of the day this was business. The last time he understood he had to come across ... no more delays." He paused. "He was to pay in cash," he added.

DeKok had listened carefully.

"What do you mean *in cash?*"

Freddie extinguished his cigarette in an ashtray.

"He offered me this gob of jewelry."

It was DeKok's turn to sit up straight in his chair.

"Jewelry?" he inquired, trying to hide any emotion.

Freddie nodded complacently.

"He wanted me to accept it as payment."

They plodded along the wide side of Gelder Quay in silence. Each was lost in his own thoughts. The statements of the gambling boss had brought yet another dimension to the murder. Vledder finally broke the silence.

"Do you really believe that Freddie wasn't interested in the jewelry?"

"Yes," nodded DeKok slowly. "Freddie Wezel is not a man to take unnecessary risks. As he said, he suspected they were hot. The moment he accepted the jewelry it would have become his responsibility. Sooner, rather than later, he'd have to convert this very distinctive property into cash. He'd have to involve middlemen ... too messy. Here's how Freddie thinks: He'd rather keep clown boy on a tight tether. You can bet Pierrot would fear Freddie more than any consequence of selling stolen jewelry."

Vledder sighed deeply.

"Trouble is we're not even sure *which* jewels we're talking about." He glanced at DeKok. "We never looked around the houseboat. Could they still be there?"

DeKok shrugged.

"I doubt Pierrot would make such a dumb move. Remember he'd already shown the jewelry to Freddie." He grinned. "Freddie is like a shark. He'd tip off one of his underworld connections to sniff around the houseboat, but only after Freddie had taken the first bite."

"You mean, after he had Pierrot's debt covered."

"Yes, of course. But it never got that far, according to Freddie. Pierrot was dead hours before Freddie's deadline." He paused and stopped suddenly. There was a thoughtful look on his face as he slowly chewed his lower lip. Then he started moving again. "I have a good idea," he continued. "Freddie did have him running scared. We can safely assume Pierrot would scramble to get the money before his time ran out."

They turned a corner and found themselves in Amsterdam's China Town.

"Where are we going?" asked Vledder. "You looking for a place to eat?"

"No," said DeKok. "It's too early, besides, I brought my lunch today. No, I thought we might as well take a look at the houseboat, since you mentioned it."

"Why?"

"Buitendam was so reluctant to make the murder a department priority. It is doubtful he'd call headquarters to ask a forensic team to examine the victim's residence. He's all about solving the robberies in The Hague. Chances are we'll find it in virgin condition, so to speak."

"Do you know where the boat is?"

"Yes, on the Inner Side, near Skipper Street."

Vledder looked apprehensive.

"How are you going to get in? I found no keys in Pierrot's clothing."

DeKok smiled. He felt in his pockets and produced a small brass tube, a little wider than a fountain pen. Handy Henkie, a former burglar and now a respectable instrument maker, had made it for DeKok. The tube contained enough picks and other unique instruments to allow DeKok to open just about any lock. Henkie had trained him well in its use.

Vledder saw what he held in his hands.

"You're not going to break in, again?" He sounded worried. "Why? The commissaris would get us a search warrant, no problem."

"No." DeKok shook his head. "I just explained. It was his job to get the forensic team to the property. That's standard operating procedure. If he had done it we'd have seen a report or gotten a phone call by now. If we ask for a warrant now, he's going to ask all sorts of questions we can't answer. We still know too little."

They reached Inner Side Canal. DeKok steered left, in the direction of Skipper Street.

"Besides," continued DeKok, "Buitendam warned me not to pursue the murder case. It puts me in a difficult position." He looked at Vledder. "If we drop the murder case, we cannot be sure Pierrot offered the jewels as payment!"

Vledder sighed in exasperation.

"Look. A search warrant *could* result in the recovery of the jewels."

DeKok was unmoved. If at all possible, he intended to keep the commissaris out of his investigation. As they reached Skipper Street, they crossed the quay. DeKok led the way across the gangplank to the front door of the houseboat. Carefully he felt the knob. The door was locked. He turned to Vledder.

"Stand close behind me. No one needs to see this."

The young inspector groaned, but shielded his partner from curious eyes.

DeKok took a closer look at the lock and selected a particular setting on his little instrument. He inserted it into the lock and twisted. Within a few seconds, the door creaked open.

They entered cautiously. DeKok quietly closed the front door behind them. They entered a hallway—to the right a door was ajar. DeKok pushed against it.

He froze in surprise as he observed the chaos in the room. In the center a table was upside down on the floor, with one leg broken. Chairs had been tossed around at random. Drawers and cupboards were open, the contents spilled on the floor.

Vledder looked over DeKok's shoulder.

"They've been here first."

DeKok walked farther into the room. Vledder followed. At the end of the room an open door led to a bedroom. Here, too, the scene was one of total chaos. The bed was upside down, the contents of the closets emptied onto the floor.

Vledder nudged DeKok and pointed at the blue, floor-length curtains. One curtain billowed as if the window behind it were open. DeKok walked to the curtains and opened them. They covered a French door, leading to a narrow deck. It stood open.

DeKok stood still and exhaled. He was too intrigued for stress. There was no sign of forcible entry. The doors looked as if they had been opened from the inside.

"Vledder, notify forensics. Get a team here as soon as possible. The commissaris cannot delay any longer. I have—" he stopped talking suddenly. He had heard a faint, squeaking nose. He motioned Vledder to come closer.

"There's somebody at the door," he whispered.

The two inspectors froze almost half a minute, then they stepped out of the bedroom, back into the living room.

A young woman stood next to an upended chair. DeKok approached her.

"Who are you?" he asked casually.

The woman was startled.

"Charlotte ..." she said.

"Fantinelli's wife," completed DeKok.

11

DeKok bowed stiffly in the direction of the young woman, while he kept his eyes glued to her face. She was very beautiful, he thought, unusually so. Tall and slender, she had charming curves. She was dressed in a formfitting overcoat. Just above her slightly elevated cheekbones, big green eyes sparkled in her oval face. Long, blonde hair descended in waves down to her shoulders.

DeKok consciously allowed himself to be swayed by his first impression. He knew her beauty had an effect on him. She emanated a provocative, tantalizing scent. She had an aura of glamour and sensuality. He realized most men would find her irresistibly enticing.

He coughed, buying a moment. It took a few more seconds for him to break the spell she had cast.

"It's a ... eh, it's a pleasure to make your acquaintance," he stuttered. "My name is DeKok, with a kay-oh-kay." He pointed at Vledder. "And this is my colleague, Vledder. We're inspectors, attached to Warmoes Street Station, and we're investigating the murder of the clown, Pierrot."

She looked confused.

"Police," she said with a sigh of relief.

DeKok gave her a penetrating look.

"You expected someone else?"

Charlotte shook her head.

"No ... no, I wasn't expecting anyone."

DeKok stretched out an index finger.

"But *we* were surprised to find you here. How did you get in?"

The young woman felt in her coat pocket and held up a key.

"Pieter and I were old friends. He gave me this key." She hesitated for a moment, looked from DeKok to Vledder, and back again. "His real name was Pieter ... Pieter Eikelbos."

"We know that," smiled DeKok.

Charlotte lifted her head.

"Are you getting anywhere?"

"With what?"

"With your investigation."

DeKok did not respond. He did not care to have someone else take the initiative in a conversation.

"Your visit here had a purpose?" he asked, harsher than it was meant to be.

She nodded.

"I came for a clean pair of pajamas, for Pieter. He's going to be buried tomorrow, and I don't want him to be buried in one of those horrible paper shrouds."

"When did you last see Pieter?"

Her expression became sad.

"Last weekend ... we spent it together, here. Sunday afternoon he left for a performance. He was to perform in Leeuwarden that night."

"And Monday night in Groningen?"

"That's right," she nodded. "Pieter was always heavily booked."

"Tell me about you and Fantinelli?"

She shook her head.

"It's been hard to find gigs since the bankruptcy."

DeKok rubbed his chin.

"That Sunday afternoon, after Pieter left, how long did you stay?"

"I had to finish his suit."

DeKok looked puzzled.

"His suit?"

"I should have said costume. Pieter always had two costumes, one spare, you see. Friday night somebody broke into his car. It was parked on the quay, in front of the boat."

"Someone stole costumes out of his car?"

"Yes, along with his make-up kit. I bought the material for the costume Saturday." She smiled. "Before I met Fantinelli I worked in a fashion house. I modeled and did alterations."

"And where is that costume now?"

Charlotte lowered her head. Her sensual aura diminished markedly. She looked stricken.

"That," she said despondently, "is the costume he wore when he was killed."

"The new suit?"

"Yes, it has to be. The costume he wore Sunday, in Leeuwarden, is still in his car."

DeKok narrowed his eyes.

"How do you know that?"

She pointed behind her.

"I looked in the trunk. The car is parked down the canal, under the trees. It isn't locked—Pieter never had time to fix the broken lock."

DeKok pondered. Clearly the clown's murder was meticulously planned and executed, right down to timing the appearance of his replacement on the stage in Groningen.

While he thought, he studied the face of the young woman. He searched feverishly for a motive.

"What was the nature of your relationship with Pieter?"

"I don't understand," she said, flustered.

DeKok searched for the right words.

"According to our information," he said hesitantly, "your, eh, your interest in men is primarily sexual."

Her eyes flashed.

"So?"

DeKok heard the combative tone in her voice.

"What I'm getting at is whether you shared—outside of the bedroom—did you also share his worries?"

"Did he have things that worried him?"

DeKok nodded emphatically.

"We know he was being pressed to pay heavy gambling debts."

Charlotte gave him a short, scornful laugh.

"What else? He was a compulsive gambler, probably for his adult life. It was well known for as long as he was a member of the theater group. He'd probably started long before that. He never had a steady relationship with a woman. He didn't want anyone to share his misery."

"He was prepared to show you the same concern?"

There was a tender smile on her face.

"I accepted him unconditionally."

"Did he respond in kind?"

Again there was a brief flashing of the eyes.

"He knew my history."

DeKok nodded soothingly.

"Did everyone in the theater group know about his gambling problems?"

Charlotte grinned.

"Pieter never made a secret of that. Whenever he won, he would be very generous—presents, dinners, drinks. When he hit a slump, he would try to borrow money from everybody."

DeKok shook his head in bewilderment.

"How could the group, then, make him responsible for the finances?"

Charlotte looked surprised.

"He did a good job. Of us all he was the most qualified. Even my husband appreciated his effectiveness. He really gave no one reason to criticize. It only started to get bad about six months ago. Suddenly, the accounts were drained. All we had left were unpaid bills."

"And you, the group, went broke."

She nodded.

"Lots of pain and misery followed ... broken contracts, no work. We had no prospects and no income."

"Did you already have an affair with Pieter at that time?"

"No, not then ... at that time I was involved with Charles, Charles Boer."

DeKok gave her a sly look.

"Was that the acrobat, or the magician?"

The sadness fled from her face. Her full lips curled into a sweet smile.

"Mr. DeKok, you have done your homework." There was a hint of admiration in her voice.

The gray sleuth ignored the remark and the compliment. He pointed at the destruction around them.

"Do have any idea who might be responsible for this mess?"

Charlotte made a helpless gesture.

"The murderer, I imagine."

DeKok did not seem to understand her.

"What could he have been looking for?"

Charlotte shrugged.

"Really, I have no idea."

The inspector concentrated on her face before he asked the next question.

"Do you know where Pieter hid the jewels?"

"Jewels?" There was genuine surprise in her voice.

"Yes."

"What jewels?"

DeKok spread his hands in a gesture of surrender.

"The jewels he wanted to use to pay off his gambling debts."

For a long time Charlotte just looked at him. Her face was expressionless. Then she pressed her lips together and shook her head. There was an alert look in her green eyes. Finally she spoke, slowly and clearly.

"Pieter has never owned any jewels."

Vledder walked angrily up and down the detective room, raking his hands through his blond hair. His face was red. Finally he stopped in front of DeKok's desk.

"She's lying," he exclaimed emotionally. He banged a full fist on DeKok's desk. "She's a liar," he repeated, "she knows very well what jewels we're talking about." He leaned on the desk and brought his face close to DeKok. "Could you not see she was lying?"

DeKok nodded.

"I heard her," he said laconically.

Vledder became even more excited.

"Yet you did *nothing* ... absolutely NOTHING. You just let her walk away, carrying the victim's pajamas."

DeKok looked up at him, while he took a sandwich out of his brown bag.

"What should I have done?" he asked sarcastically. "Should I have interrogated her? Put her on the rack ... flogged her ... pulled out her nails? Just tell me what you wanted."

Vledder ignored the sarcasm. He pulled up a chair and sank down in it.

"This reeks, DeKok," he said, more even-tempered. "It stinks like rot."

"What? My sandwich? You want one? My wife packed an extra one. It's prosciutto—no stink."

Vledder shook his head impatiently.

"You're not getting it. Charlotte is in this up to her neck. You saw her. She's one of those women, who are irresistibly drawn to crime."

DeKok managed to look surprised as he took a bite from his sandwich.

"What's that?" he asked with his mouth full. "Psycho-babble?"

Vledder shook his head.

"You know very well there is a type," he said, irritation in his voice. "In this line of work we meet them. Matter of fact, weren't you the one who said, 'The more beautiful the woman, the greater her capacity for getting into trouble?'"

"And Charlotte is in trouble?"

"Here we go again," nodded Vledder "Fantinelli is our man. He used Clarisse, or Carol—whatever her name is—to get the information he needed to organize the robbery at Vlaanderen's. Charlotte heard about it from Carol. Charlotte told Pierrot. Pierrot, in financial need and under threat by Freddie and Company, demanded a part of the loot."

DeKok rocked slowly back and forth in his chair.

"I see," he said, "so while they were discussing this delicate subject, a fight erupted. Fantinelli shoved one of his knives between Pierrot's ribs."

Vledder slapped his hand down on his own knee.

"Exactly, that's a wrap." It sounded like a challenge.

DeKok thoughtfully swallowed the last of his sandwich and lifted his coffee mug. Then he put it down and lifted an index finger into the air.

"Now, however, Charlotte wants nothing whatsoever to do with the jewelry."

Vledder grinned crookedly.

"Understandable," he said with fervor. "She would be stupid to open her mouth at this time. Pierrot is dead. There's nothing left to get from a dead lover. Based on her history, we know she can fall back into the loving arms of her husband anytime she wishes."

DeKok took a sip of coffee and then smiled derisively.

"A very good financial prospect, which Fantinelli richly endowed with a fortune in antique jewelry."

"Exactly," agreed Vledder. "If I read Charlotte right, and I think I did, she'll return to Fantinelli full of remorse, teary-eyed. She probably has already done so." He paused and frowned. "It wouldn't be a bit surprising if Carol became Fantinelli's next victim."

DeKok stared at him in amazement.

"Carol?"

"Don't you see, DeKok?" cried Vledder, full of excitement. "As it stands now, Carol is the only witness against the Fantinellis ... and they could take her cut."

"You mean," said DeKok, "if the Fantinellis split the proceeds as husband and wife, they share with no one."

Vledder looked triumphant.

"Now you're getting it. It falls together naturally."

DeKok leaned forward.

"Eh, didn't you say you had rejected the theory of Carol's involvement in the theft? Just checking—now you've changed your mind?"

"Yes," said Vledder confidently. "I've been mulling it over. When she was here, she acted the innocent. That's all it was … just an act. Something about her demeanor made me change my mind. Anyway without Carol in the equation, there's no solution. She is the *only* one who could get access to Vlaanderen's safe."

DeKok drained his coffee mug and stood up. He could not accept the notion of Carol as an accomplice. It was plain unthinkable, despite Vledder's convictions. For a moment he seemed to wonder what to do next. Then he walked over to get his coat and hat.

Vledder got up and followed.

"Where are you headed?"

"I'm going to ask Henri Jonkers what he knows about jewelry."

At that moment the telephone on DeKok's desk rang. Vledder walked back and picked up the receiver.

DeKok waited. He watched Vledder's back while he talked on the phone. Instinctively he knew it was an important call. Vledder turned around, the receiver still in his hand. There was a haunted look on his face.

"Butterfly."

"What about Butterfly?"

"She's been found in her apartment."

"Murdered?"

"Yes," said Vledder. "There was a knife in her back."

12

Intently crouched over the steering wheel, Vledder concentrated on guiding his VW through the heavy traffic. In a few minutes DeKok observed at least thirteen serious traffic violations. He gave his partner an irritated look.

"What are you doing? You're driving as if the devil is behind you. You're always in such a hurry to reach a corpse. Do you think it will walk away?"

Vledder pressed harder on the accelerator.

"The bastard."

"Who?"

"How could anyone sink low enough to kill such a little girl," replied Vledder sharply.

DeKok straightened up in the seat. To head off a fruitless conversation, he changed the subject.

"What, exactly, did the watch commander say ... who was killed? Butterfly or Martha Hagen?"

"Butterfly."

DeKok sighed and sank back in his seat. For the rest of the trip he was lost in his own thoughts.

A young, uniformed constable guarded the door to the apartment building. He saluted politely when DeKok approached.

"You came fast," he said.

"Anybody else here?"

The constable shook his head.

"No, we reported to the watch commander. He said he would inform you. Whether he notified anyone else, I don't know. My partner is upstairs, the third floor. He's taking a statement from the neighbor who found her."

"How was the body discovered?"

"The neighbor was going out for an errand. When he passed her door he noticed it was ajar. He thought it strange. He knew the victim as a shy woman, who was seldom out. She always kept her doors and windows closed."

"So he took a look?"

"He said he called out before going in. When there was no answer, he entered the apartment. He found her in the living room and knew at once she was dead. He says he didn't touch anything, but went back upstairs to call the police."

DeKok nodded his understanding.

"And you got the call by radio?"

"Yes."

"What was the message?"

"Proceed immediately to Patrick Henry Street, number 764, second floor. Report of a dead woman. Possible homicide."

Vledder understood that the constable was translating the coded message as he went along. Apparently even this young constable knew DeKok's reputation. DeKok abhorred codes. But then, he hated anything to do with radio communications. The radio in the VW was almost always turned off. He stubbornly refused to carry a personal radio. It was somewhere in the trunk, gathering dust.

"That was the whole message?"

"That was it."

Vledder was getting impatient. He tried to enter the building behind DeKok's back, but his old colleague motioned for him to wait while he continued the conversation with the constable.

"So," he recapitulated, "you drove here, established that the woman was indeed murdered, and asked your watch commander to contact Homicide?"

"Yes, that's it."

DeKok rubbed his chin.

"Where did you get the name *Butterfly?*"

The constable pointed upstairs.

"The neighbor ... he said that was what the woman was called."

She was in a prone position, her upper body on the seat of the couch where the two inspectors had been seated during their previous visit. Her lower legs and knees rested on the carpet. From her back protruded a throwing knife of the same model that had been used on the clown.

DeKok leaned over her. Her narrow, oval face was turned to one side. Both eyes were half closed and her mouth was frozen in a bitter smile. It was as though she had always known what would happen to her.

He took another look at the knife. Just as with the clown, the knife had penetrated the tiny body for the length of the blade. There was less blood. He looked up at Vledder, who stood across from the body. The young man was obviously trying to control his emotions. Both hands were balled into fists, the white showing around his knuckles. His face was pale and there was a nervous tic along his jaw.

DeKok saw it with concern and pity. Whenever death presented itself in its gruesome inevitability, he had the same feeling of anger and helplessness. But over the years he had learned to outwardly control his emotions. It gave him the strength to appear unmoved, to do his job objectively. The nightmares didn't come until later.

Vledder moved and came to stand next to DeKok. With a shaking hand he pointed at the slight, delicate shape of the dead woman.

"This ..." he said in a shaking voice, "this should never have happened. Surely we could have prevented this. We should never have given the killer this opportunity. We, we're also guilty."

DeKok listened, primarily, to the sad tone of his voice. He was annoyed by the self-accusation.

"How are we culpable?" he exclaimed angrily. "Are you a clairvoyant? Am I? How do you expect to produce a murderer just like that?" He snapped his fingers. "Are we magicians? Do we pull them out of a high hat like rabbits?"

He felt the anger taking hold of him. Despite his years of experience and his customary iron self-control, he felt the berserker rage growing. This rage slumbers in every placid Dutchman. It is a national trait, some say a curse. With difficulty he took a deep breath and finally succeeded in calming himself.

"I know, before God," he continued, in a more reasonable tone of voice, "I know I've done the best I can. If this murderer is quicker or smarter than I, he's only ahead of me for now."

Vledder appeared to not have heard a word.

DeKok studied the tall, young man. He bent his head, his shoulders sloped. He had the aura of defeat. It was all slightly odious to DeKok. With a sudden, stern gesture he pointed at the door.

"Alert the Herd," he ordered. "Then tell that guy on the floor above, who recalled his neighbor's stage name with such precision, we'll expect him at Warmoes Street no later than eight o'clock this evening."

Vledder hastily left the room. He appeared to be escaping.

DeKok watched him go. In a complete reversal of feelings he wondered whether, somehow, he had failed his young partner. He pushed the distressing thought into his subconscious and looked around the room. Things looked much the same as they did on their previous visit. He remembered the leather chairs and the hassock on which she had been seated. He dredged the scene from his memory—how she looked, the prim gesture when she covered her knees.

Poor Butterfly, indeed. What had she known? Why would anyone wish her dead? There had to be a motive. Where was the sense in forever silencing this diminutive woman? Was she perhaps *the* Butterfly who lingered in the memory of Julius Vlaanderen, the broker who seemed to have started it all?

He rubbed the bridge of his nose. There was one confrontation he still had to arrange. It could be done, even if it was with death. Stupid not to have thought of it before.

He stepped back and observed the scene from a distance. The large throwing knife in her back looked horrifying and obscene. The knife seemed almost larger than the frail figure below it. He would never forget this. It was even more intrusive and memorable than the picture of the clown. He tried to revive his sluggish thought processes. Was Martha Hagen killed because she was Martha Hagen? Or was it her stage persona who held the key to the motive? The thoughts tumbled through his head, but he could not close the circuit. It was as though the individual thoughts were arranged in a three-dimensional puzzle, nearly impossible to connect.

A noise on the landing interrupted his thoughts. Bram Weelen entered the room a second later he was followed by Ben Kruger. Both carried aluminum suitcases. They were the first of the Herd, as DeKok frequently called the small army who always gathered at the scene of a murder.

"You're amazingly quick," DeKok said by way of greeting. "It must be a record. Were you waiting around the corner?"

Weelen grinned.

"No, we took the call in the car. We happened to be sharing a cruiser, on our way back from a job in West Harbor. A Greek cook on a tramp steamer was found hanging between his pots and pans. The crew didn't like his cooking."

"You're making that up," accused DeKok.

"No. True. No joke. The Water Police are handling the case."

Ben Kruger walked around DeKok and got a good look at the corpse.

"Well, I'll be," he said. "That's the same knife we found in that clown."

DeKok shook his head.

"That's impossible. It is the same *type* of knife. The knife that killed the clown is in my desk at the station."

Kruger looked bland.

"That's what I meant," he said. "It's *like* that knife." He leaned over the victim. "How many of those knives are floating around?"

DeKok spread his hands.

"About a month ago a whole set was stolen from the car of a knife thrower in Apeldoorn."

"How many in a set?"

"Twelve."

Weelen grimaced.

"So, you can expect another ten murders?"

DeKok looked baffled.

"Surely you don't really think," he said, "that the killer is going to use all the knives?"

Weelen waved at the corpse.

"If you ask me he's working at it."

Kruger slapped Weelen on the shoulder.

"Hurry up," he admonished. "Take your pictures so I can start with my brush." He pointed at the dead woman and turned to DeKok. "Is she in our collection?"

DeKok shook his head.

"No, you'll have to take her prints. Vledder checked it. She's not in our files."

"You know her?"

DeKok nodded slowly.

"I talked with her only yesterday."

"She's somehow connected with the murder of the clown?"

"Yes."

Kruger looked at the corpse.

"Perhaps that is what scared the killer."

DeKok gave him an admiring look.

"Ben," he said, "you're such an old pro." He turned around. Dr. Koning was in the door opening. Behind him were the ubiquitous morgue attendants.

DeKok approached the old coroner with his hands spread wide in a gesture of apology.

"I'm sorry, doctor," he said, "But I have to bother you again."

Dr. Koning took off his old Garibaldi hat and looked at DeKok with a mocking look in his eyes.

"Don't apologize, old friend," he said, shaking his head. "As long as crime flourishes, we can't really retire."

He did not wait for a reaction from DeKok, but walked toward the dead woman. Once again, his examination took longer than DeKok recalled. The coroner leaned close to the corpse and examined it from every angle. After a long time, he closed her eyes and with some difficulty came to a standing position.

"She is dead."

It sounded laconic. DeKok nodded with resignation.

"I feared so."

The old coroner took out a large handkerchief and wiped his glasses. Meanwhile he inclined his head in the direction of the corpse.

"I think it happened last night, or maybe this morning, very early."

"Rigor is complete?"

Dr. Koning nodded. He replaced his handkerchief and his pince-nez. He looked at the ceiling.

"Did you notice the position of her hands?"

DeKok narrowed his eyes.

"What's the matter with her hands? They aren't visible."

"They're folded under her chest."
DeKok was startled.
"Folded?"
Dr. Koning nodded.
"She was praying when she was killed."

13

Vledder was so surprised that he involuntarily twisted the steering wheel around and almost rammed a parked car.

"Praying?" he asked, incredulous.

DeKok nodded slowly.

"According to the coroner, Butterfly was kneeling in prayer when she was killed."

"She was on her knees," agreed Vledder.

"With folded hands."

"I didn't see that."

"I didn't either, at first. Her hands were hidden beneath her chest. Actually, I did not look as closely as Dr. Koning did when he came. It wasn't until the morgue attendants lifted her up that I saw her folded hands, the fingers entwined."

Vledder looked somber. His face still had little color.

"After I alerted the Herd, I went to see the neighbor on the third floor. I told him to be at the station by eight o'clock. After that, I sat down in the car. I'm sorry, DeKok, really ... but I just couldn't go back to that room."

"I noticed. Kruger missed you as well."

"What did you tell him?"

"I just said you weren't feeling well."

Vledder shook his head.

"It wasn't that," he said hotly. "You know that."

DeKok allowed himself to sink down in his seat. His face was expressionless.

"No worries," he said tiredly. "I wouldn't attempt to justify it. But I can understand. Butterfly made the same impression on me. I thought her to be a sweet, good-natured young woman. Finding her one day later with a knife ..." He did not complete the sentence. "This is a dirty job at times. We have to steel ourselves. A professional should be able to objectively investigate the murder of his own mother."

Vledder looked wild.

"Could you do that?" he demanded.

DeKok shook his head sadly. He sank lower in his seat. The mere thought of his old mother as the victim of a horrible crime made him shiver.

"No, I don't believe I could," he said finally. "Objectivity is overrated. Objective people often keep their emotional distance, loosing their humanity in the process. Humanity should be the primary requisite for a policeman. Without it, we would be machines—heartless, soulless automatons." He paused. "No," he added, "that would never do."

After that they drove for a while in silence. Vledder was the first one to speak again.

"Is there some significance to the praying attitude?"

"Yes."

"That she was praying?"

"No."

Vledder was surprised.

"Not praying?" he exclaimed. "But Dr Koning said ..." he swallowed. "You say you saw it yourself. Her fingers were entwined."

DeKok pushed himself up so that he could at least look over the dashboard.

"It's not natural," he said, shaking his head. "Nobody maintains a praying position while being violently stabbed in the back. Therefore I disagree with Dr. Koning. She was not in that position when she was killed. We have seen that once before, you'll remember." He thought for a moment. "It was that case you called 'The Brothers of the Easy Death.' Remember, we found drowned couples with their hands entwined. They had apparently committed double suicides. Later we found out we didn't have the answer."

"Yes, I remember that case," said Vledder. "It was sometime ago, you—"

DeKok interrupted.

"Besides, I don't think our little Butterfly was all that religious. It doesn't seem she would pray to Our Dear Lord on her bare knees. I did not see a Bible, statue, or religious text anywhere in that apartment."

Vledder now became derisive.

"But her hands were folded in prayer."

"Exactly," agreed DeKok. "It was supposed to look like a praying posture. Somebody placed her body in that position."

"But who?"

"The murderer, of course."

"And why?"

DeKok glanced at Vledder. He was relieved to see his partner's face had regained its normal coloration.

"Why," he began hesitantly, "would someone put a dead clown in a conspicuous white suit on a small dock near Gelder Quay?"

Vledder parked the VW behind the station house. As

DeKok unfolded himself to exit the car he looked at his watch. Then he compared it with the large clock on Central Station across the water. It was almost fifteen minutes past eight o'clock. The realization spurred him on. With a buoyant step he turned into Old Bridge Alley to reach Warmoes Street. Vledder followed with long strides. It wasn't often he had to hurry to keep up with his partner. They reached the front door of the station together. As they passed the counter that divides the lobby, Kuster called out to them.

"There's a magician waiting for you."

As if thunderstruck, DeKok halted in his stride. Then he walked over to the counter.

"A magician?"

The watch commander nodded.

"He said he was supposed to be here at eight o'clock."

DeKok narrowed his eyes.

"Did he tell you he was a magician?"

Kuster shook his head.

"No, he just said he was expected at eight o'clock. Said it was in connection with the murder of a woman on Patrick Henry Street. But I recognized him. In my spare time I'm treasurer of an amateur soccer club. He performed at one of our parties."

"As a magician?"

Kuster nodded.

"What an event! We had a high-wire act, a ventriloquist, a knife thrower, a clown, an acrobat, a hypnotist, a magician ... you know what I mean?"

"How long ago was this?"

Kuster looked at the ceiling while he thought.

"It was our twenty-fifth anniversary. That was about a year and a half ago."

A man was seated on the bench along the third floor corridor, across from the detective room. DeKok studied him intently. He estimated the man to be in his early thirties. He had a handsome face, non-Dutch, perhaps southern European, with olive tone skin and black, shiny hair. His nose was slightly bent. A Roman nose, thought DeKok.

As soon as the man saw Vledder, he stood up and approached them.

"I was on time," he said in an arrogant voice. It sounded like a rebuke.

Vledder's eyes flashed angrily

"We weren't," he said curtly.

DeKok hastily intervened.

"Our apologies," he said, simply. He led the man into the detective room. "We got stuck in traffic. Traffic in Amsterdam is getting to be a regular jungle, regardless of the hour."

The man looked at the old detective.

"Just the traffic?" he asked nastily. "All of Amsterdam is a jungle, a criminal jungle. You people aren't doing anything to change it."

DeKok saw that Vledder was about to burst out. Silently he warned him to be quiet. DeKok turned to the man and smiled.

"We'll try to change your opinion of our efforts," he said politely. "But you must also take into consideration the obstacles we face. Amsterdam is a compassionate city for law-abiding citizens ... also for criminals."

The man snorted.

"Compassionate, compassionate ... how compassionate was Pieter's murderer?"

DeKok seated the man on the chair next to his desk.

"Pieter ... which Pieter would that be?"

The man gesticulated.

"Pieter Eikelbos, the clown. And now Butterfly. Don't you get it? Someone is after our group."

DeKok merely looked at the man.

"And what group would that be?"

"Our group—the Variety Troupe, if you want to be exact."

"Oh, *that* group. And you're a member as well?"

The man nodded.

"As the magician."

DeKok picked up the statement taken by the constable in the man's apartment.

"You're Frans Heid?"

"Yes."

"It says here you live on the floor above the murdered woman."

The magician sighed.

"Yes, I used to live in a rooming house. When I joined the group, Butterfly arranged for me to rent an apartment in her building."

"I had an opportunity to review the statement you made to the police this afternoon. There is no mention of your membership in the Variety Troupe, a group, I might add, to which Butterfly belonged, as well."

The magician lowered his head.

"I didn't want to mention that, at first. I thought it would look suspicious when I happened to discover the murder."

"Why?"

"Relationships within the group were sometimes difficult. There were, and there still are, disagreements. These quarrels could easily be interpreted to my disadvantage."

"Such as?"

The magician grimaced, as if in pain, while he rubbed the back of neck.

"I ... eh, I ... had a relationship with Charlotte, Fantinelli's wife. Butterfly wanted me to end the affair. She contrived to have Fantinelli catch Charlotte and me in a compromising situation. Her meddling infuriated me. I was very vocal about it."

"You made threats?"

"Indeed. They were idle threats, made in the heat of the moment. It was a lot of noise, but no substance. Afterwards I was sorry about it."

DeKok leaned back in his chair and pulled on his earlobe.

"Was Martha's door really open this afternoon?" he asked.

The magician did not answer, but looked at DeKok silently. The silence lasted almost a minute. DeKok merely waited.

"No," the magician said finally. "I opened the door."

"You have a key?"

"Yes."

"And ... you had an affair, a relationship with Butterfly?"

The magician shook his head.

"No, we were just ... friends. That's all. She gave me a key, some time ago, so I could take care of her cat when she was away."

DeKok leaned forward.

"How much jewelry did Butterfly have?"

"What jewelry?" Heid asked sharply.

"Antique jewelry."

The magician shrugged.

"I've never seen any. She was crazy about onyx. She had some jewelry with onyx, but no more than a woman would normally have."

"What made you change your mind?"

"I don't understand."

DeKok smiled slyly.

"Why are you much more forthcoming than this afternoon?"

The man made a tired gesture.

"I realized right away the officer downstairs remembered my magic act."

"That is the only reason?"

Frans Heid nodded slowly.

"I, eh, I …" he said softly, "I could have kept my discovery of the body to myself. It would have been easy to leave and act as though I hadn't seen a thing. The sight of Butterfly with that big throwing knife in her back compelled me. I called the police hoping my connections with the group would not be an issue." He swallowed. "It was very tempting to get out of Amsterdam."

DeKok gave him a searching look.

"Why?"

The magician turned his head away. The olive color of his skin was a sallow grey. He remained silent.

This time DeKok did not wait for an answer.

"Why?" he repeated.

Frans Heid licked his dry lips.

"Do you know how many people were members of our group?"

"Not precisely."

"Twelve. And do you know how many knives Fantinelli lost?"

"Twelve," said DeKok.

The magician's eyes were large and scared.

"Inspector, I'm afraid."

14

DeKok had tired feet. That is what he called the onslaught of his private torment. Suddenly, there they were, unannounced. It was like a sudden squall on a perfectly calm sea. He leaned back and placed his feet carefully on the corner of his desk. He leaned forward and felt his calves, his face contorted with pain. Surprisingly the pain was never accompanied by inflammation. His legs felt as if a thousand little devils were poking him with red-hot pitchforks. The pain was all too familiar. His physician assured him over and over again it was purely psychosomatic. No examinations or tests had revealed any organic cause. This came as no consolation, even once he knew what triggered these episodes. Whenever a case was progressing badly, when no solution was in sight, the pain began. He realized this had occurred because he was flailing about helplessly. As always, the darkness surrounded him and the little demons promptly appeared to torment him.

Vledder also knew the symptoms. He looked at his partner with a concerned face.

"Feet hurting?" he asked.

DeKok nodded and closed his eyes. He remained motionless and focused for several minutes. His usually animated face became a steel mask.

"It's easing," he said wanly. "The pain is just bearable.

What makes it intolerable is the knowledge that after two murders and several days we have made no progress. Worse, I have a bad feeling, a premonition."

Vledder looked stunned.

"You cannot believe we're not going to be able to solve this?" he asked anxiously.

DeKok looked him straight in the eye before he answered.

"It's possible. Many murders are never solved."

Vledder shook his head emphatically.

"We solve ours. I mean *you* solve yours. As long as we have worked together we have never lost a case. We never give up—it's, it's just not in the cards."

DeKok smiled suddenly.

"Maybe it's my superstitious side coming out."

"How do you mean?"

"My tired feet couldn't have anything to do with the progress of the case."

Vledder laughed, relieved.

"Exactly, and we'll get past it." He pushed his chair closer to DeKok's desk. "What about the magician's story? His fear seemed genuine. He is convinced the murderer plans to wipe out that entire variety group. What do you believe?"

DeKok hesitated. He rubbed his legs and stared out of the window.

"Here's a remarkable coincidence. Bram Weelen said as much this afternoon. When I told Weelen twelve identical knives had been stolen from a car in Apeldoorn, he said, 'So, you can expect another ten murders.'"

"Okay, but do you agree?"

"Cops have to be prepared for all sorts of twisted

minds. Human behavior isn't always predictable. Peoples' motives are complex. Some people behave in an aberrant manner. People kill people whose faces they don't like." He fell silent and then suddenly grinned boyishly. "Because I must justify my attitude towards the commissaris, I'm going with the theory that these two murders are connected to the jewel theft."

Vledder nodded thoughtfully.

"And Butterfly is connected to all that."

DeKok lowered his feet from the desk. He stood up and tried a few steps. With a relieved sigh he sat down again. Then he pointed a finger at Vledder.

"The autopsy is at eleven in the morning. On the way, pick up old man Vlaanderen. Show him Martha's corpse before they start cutting. Perhaps it will jog his memory. It's worth a try."

"And if he doesn't want to come?"

"I'll give him a call before that time." He looked at the clock. "You know what I feel like?"

"At least one glass of good cognac?" smiled Vledder.

"You read my mind."

Little Lowee's face lit up with pleasure when he saw DeKok enter his intimate bar. He greeted the gray sleuth jovially.

"Well come," he chirped. "Din'ta knowed you hadda time."

DeKok hoisted himself onto a barstool. Vledder followed his example.

"If you forget the little pleasures of life," said DeKok, "you forget to live."

Little Lowee looked sad.

"Mokum done goin' backward, I thinks. There ain't alotta pleasures left."

DeKok looked surprised.

"You are becoming pessimistic, Lowee. I'm not used to that."

"I hear them maggots got Butterfly."

It was DeKok's turn to look sad.

"Again with a throwing knife."

"You gotta lead?"

DeKok shook his head.

"I'm just as far as the night that the clown was killed."

Lowee stared unhappily at the counter, a bottle of cognac in one hand, while his other hand moved to pick up three snifters.

"Sucha good lookin' broad. You gotta be a real bottom feeder to—" he stopped and looked up. "Same recipe?"

Without waiting for an answer, he quickly placed the snifters in a row and opened the bottle. Almost in the same movement he poured a generous measure in each glass.

"Found out anything about the jewelry?"

"Zip," answered Lowee as he picked up one of the glasses and rocked it slowly in his hand. "I done some checkin', after youse left last time, but notta whisper. I tole 'em I were innerested in them glimmers ... even the fox."

"And?"

"Nuttin', notta peep. I gotta a guy that says he hears about some jools inna houseboat. He was gonna let me know."

DeKok looked up.

"In a houseboat?"

"Yep."

"Who was that?"

Lowee looked pained.

"Don't, DeKok. I ain't spill no names. I gotta think of me reputazie."

DeKok did not urge him.

"You talked to him later?"

"Yep. He lost the tune—say it wasn't for real."

DeKok grinned.

"Tell him from me, next time he should be a bit neater. Man, oh man, he made a real mess in that boat."

The barkeep looked suspiciously.

"You'se know abouta boat?"

DeKok nodded, then took a sip from his glass. He took the time to savor the drink.

"Yes," he said after he swallowed. "The boat belongs to the murdered clown."

"Did he have them jools?"

"Some people thought he did."

Little Lowee rested his elbows on the bar.

"Somebody snuffed the clown for 'em?"

"Possibly."

"But you ain't sure?"

DeKok took another sip.

"Lowee," he said after he enjoyed his next mouthful, "I can't tell you all my secrets."

The small barkeeper took no offense.

"You knows, DeKok, it's sorta weird, you knows."

"What?"

Lowee took a quick look around. Then he leaned closer.

"Them troop, you knows, them that gone broke. I hears they owe big bucks all over. But they ain't doing so bad, you knows."

"Who?"

"Them artists. You takes that Charlie Boer, the acrobat. He just open a new sports school. Whatchamacallit—a fitness center. Gots all sorta machines and acrobatic ... aerobic dancing. I went by there and it looks just fine." He fell silent and replaced his empty glass on the counter. "I bumps into his negozie."

"Well?"

"That dame ... Charlotte."

DeKok almost choked on his cognac.

"Charlotte?"

Lowee nodded with emphasis.

"Look like she sank some loot in Charlie's binnez."

The two inspectors walked from Lowee's bar toward Rear Fort Canal and from there back to Old Acquaintance Alley. The quarter was buzzing, as always.

DeKok looked at his partner.

"Something bothering you?"

Vledder's face was dark and brooding, as though a thundercloud hung over his head.

"How crazy is this," he barked. "Every time I get a grip on the connections, new ones pop up. How many separate cases can we pursue?"

DeKok pushed on his hat. It balanced precariously close on the back of his head.

"Well, a few things are clear. The clown, Pierrot, had, or believed he had, access to valuable jewelry. He offered it to Freddie Wezel to pay off his gambling debts. Freddie refused—gave him an ultimatum, a deadline. Just before the deadline, somebody murdered the clown."

"Yes," added Vledder, "then Freddie alerted some guy about the possible whereabouts of the jewelry, and got him to ransack the houseboat."

"Exactly, but nothing turned up. One of two things happened. Either the guy didn't look hard enough, or the jewels weren't there. Personally my money's on the latter."

"Why?"

DeKok grinned.

"Think about the seeming chaos on the boat. Whoever turned that houseboat inside out, really did a number. It was a mess, but very systematic. Remember the broken leg on the table? He broke one off, found it wasn't hollow, and tried more likely hiding places. He wouldn't have missed anything." He narrowed his eyes for a moment. "There is of course, a third possibility."

"What?"

"He did find the jewels but, for whatever reason, passed Lowee by."

"Another fence?"

DeKok stopped walking and stood shaking his head.

"No," he said as he again picked up the pace. "No, I don't think so. Even though Lowee's world is dicey, Lowee is known as an *honest* fence. He pays a fair price. No," he concluded, "I have to stay with my original conviction. There were no jewels on the boat."

Vledder threw his arms up.

"What I don't get is why Pierrot tried to pay Freddie with jewelry?"

"That's the best question that's been asked during this entire investigation."

Vledder shook his head.

"Means nothing to me," he said sharply. "It's the answer I want. Let's stop overlooking the most likely possibility."

"And what is that?"

"The murderer got the jewelry—he killed Pierrot for it."

DeKok leaned his head to one side.

"How does Butterfly fit into the equation?"

His eyes were downcast, his voice smaller. "She doesn't, not yet, anyway."

DeKok smiled.

"No matter. It's still a mess … for me, too. Do you find it remarkable nobody in that group knows a thing about the jewels? Charlotte, who was closest to the clown, swears he had no jewels. Butterfly has no jewelry, except a few personal pieces. She is clueless about any other jewelry. Finally the magician looks dumbfounded when you mention the word jewelry. Yet—"

They had reached the station. As they entered, Kuster waved them closer.

"One of you call Kruger? He has something."

Vledder went behind the counter and lifted the receiver off a telephone.

DeKok took Kuster by the lapels of his coat.

"How would you like to organize another party for your soccer club, complete with variety entertainers?"

Kuster grinned.

"Are you paying?"

Vledder pushed Kuster aside. His face was serious.

"What's the matter?" asked DeKok.

"Kruger found some prints in Butterfly's apartment."

"Sounds right. Whose prints are they?"

"Maurice Vlaanderen's."

15

"How is that possible?"

Vledder looked at DeKok with a bewildered look on his face.

"What?"

"How could Kruger identify Maurice Vlaanderen's prints in her apartment, or anywhere else? Is he in our files?"

Vledder nodded.

"Maurice was caught in a theft, not a robbery, when he was eighteen. He got a suspended sentence and the file was sealed. Obviously the prints remained in our records."

"What kind of theft?"

"Jewelry."

Defeated, DeKok sank back in his chair.

"Do we need this?"

Vledder pushed his keyboard to one side and leaned closer to DeKok's desk.

"Does that change our plans? I mean, do you still want me to pick up Vlaanderen before the autopsy?"

DeKok nodded slowly, more to himself than to Vledder.

"It seems to me it could be productive, but keep it quiet. Not a word to the old man about his son's fingerprints."

"I promise," said Vledder. Then he gave DeKok a penetrating look. "When are we going to arrest Maurice?"

DeKok did not answer. It seemed he had not even heard the question. He was absorbed in trying to fit the broker's son into the big picture, to no avail. This was one thing too many. Then, proving that he had heard him after all, he spoke to Vledder.

"My conclusions are incomplete. Watch carefully for Vlaanderen's reaction when he sees Butterfly's corpse. I'll wait here in the morning. Let me know as soon as you can."

"Why don't you come along? You are more of an expert at reading people's reactions than me."

DeKok shook his head.

"Don't forget to bring me the knife from her back. I need it." He pulled open a drawer in his desk and took out the knife that had killed Pierrot. He studied it carefully. "I have some calls to make tomorrow. Among others I want to talk to the Water Police."

"What about?"

"I want to know if they found a boat."

"What kind of boat?"

"I don't know, some sort of runabout ... something with an outboard motor. I'll have to check."

"I see," said Vledder. He wondered whether DeKok's knowledge of boats was as limited as his knowledge of cars.

DeKok looked at the wall clock. He hoisted himself out of his chair and grabbed his raincoat off its peg.

"I'm going home. It's almost eleven o'clock. I've had enough for one day."

"What do you want with a boat?" asked Vledder.

"Well, Dick, how do you think the clown's corpse got to that little dock? He didn't fly."

Adjutant Kamper propped open the door with one foot and stepped into the detective room. He carried an enormous stack of files in his arms. He stopped at DeKok's desk and dropped the stack.

DeKok looked up.

"What's the meaning of this?" he asked, annoyed.

The adjutant shrugged.

"The commissaris personally instructed me to bring you these. He said to put them on your desk. These are case files from The Hague concerning jewelry thefts."

DeKok shook his head sadly.

"He couldn't give them to me himself?"

Kamper grinned.

"Buitendam said he tried, but you forgot to take them with you." He turned around and whistled a tune as he walked away.

The inspector pushed the pile of papers to the outermost corner of his desk. There was a stubborn look on his face.

"Whatever you think," he growled to himself, "you're not going to read a single word."

He pulled the telephone closer and dialed a number. Angrily he tossed the receiver back on the hook. It was the sixth time he was connected to a busy signal. He tried again, but looked up when Vledder stormed into the room.

Vledder was gray around the gills. As he arrived at DeKok's desk, he dropped a plastic evidence bag, containing a bloody knife.

"Here—your souvenir."

"You don't look so good."

Vledder sank into his chair.

"It's the worst autopsy I've ever witnessed. But-terfly—Martha—was a gorgeous woman, even on the dissection table."

DeKok ignored the remark.

"Did the senior Vlaanderen recognize her?"

Vledder shook his head.

"He looked at her for a long time, outwardly unmoved. I tried to read him. He turned to me and said the woman was completely unknown to him." He sighed. "One other thing."

"What?"

"I asked Vlaanderen if Maurice would be home in the afternoon. You understand it would be handy to know his whereabouts, if we're going to arrest him."

"And?"

"Maurice never came home last night. Our bird flew the coop."

DeKok ambled over to where he kept his coat and struggled into it. Vledder called from his desk.

"Shouldn't we send out an APB before we leave?"

"What kind of APB?"

"For the apprehension of Maurice Vlaanderen."

DeKok shook his head and put on his hat.

"Wait until I get back."

Vledder looked strange.

"You're going alone?" There was a mixture of surprise and disappointment in his voice.

"Yes."

"Where are you going?"

"I'm attending Pierrot's funeral. I want to know who else shows up."

"What do you want me to do in the meantime?"

DeKok pointed at his desk.

"I checked with the Water Police this morning. They have indeed found a speedboat they can't identify. They towed it from Western Basin to their headquarters at West Dock Quay. Go take a look at that boat. I think it was used to transport Pierrot's corpse."

"From where?"

"From the houseboat on Inner Side Canal."

"So you think he was murdered at home?" Vledder seemed surprised.

"Yes," said DeKok. "Now that Lowee's friend made such a mess, we have little, if any, useful evidence. Check it out anyway, would you? Forensics should be finished with their investigation by now. Maybe they found something, maybe not."

"I'll take care of that. When will you be back?"

DeKok grinned sadly.

"After my final salute to the clown."

Outside a dense cover of low-hanging clouds covered the city. Sparse droplets of cold drizzle turned into heavy fog. Next it would change to the consistency of the "misters" one sees at amusement parks on hot days. Every once in a while it would rain harder, but never enough to warrant an umbrella. This kind of weather could keep on for days in Amsterdam, soaking everything. It looked as though Heaven had turned away from the city, leaving behind this dismal, wet blanket.

DeKok pulled up the collar of his coat and pushed his hat low down over his eyes. He moved across the gravel paths of the cemetery, in his typical duck-footed gait. The water dripped from his face. He wondered if anyone else would show up.

Anyone could have recognized his car by the way he had parked. It was an inexpert, crooked job. No other cars arrived. This surprised him; he hoped there would be other mourners to accompany Pierrot to his last resting place. He had never known the clown in life. He only remembered him in death.

The cemetery was a sad and deserted place. The flowers had lost their color and even the birds were silent. DeKok walked on, his head bent down. When he looked up he saw a woman in the distance. She stood remote and alone, under the chapel overhang. The sight stirred memories. He'd seen such great sadness too many times in his life.

When he came closer, a smile of recognition curled his lips.

"Charlotte, I'm glad to see you." It sounded sincere.

She looked around and smiled sadly.

"I thought there would be more interest. It's his last performance."

A large hearse approached at a disrespectful speed. The car stopped near the chapel. The brakes squealed and gravel flew. A man in a black uniform stepped out of the car and ran toward DeKok and Charlotte.

"You're here for Mr. Eikelbos?"

Both of them nodded.

"Oh," the man said. It sounded disappointed. "You may follow us." He ran back through the rain and slid behind the wheel.

Slowly the car moved off. Charlotte and DeKok followed. They walked silently next to each other. The gleaming, black vehicle purred softly in front of them.

Charlotte glanced aside.

"Is it usual for a police inspector to attend the funeral of a victim?"

DeKok shook his head solemnly.

"No, I came on my own."

"Why?"

The gray sleuth shrugged his shoulders.

"I had a nebulous thought," he said absent mindedly, "that few people would show up. For most people a clown and a funeral are incongruent concepts. A clown doesn't die and isn't buried. A clown just disappears, applause following him out of the ring, or off the stage," he licked his lips and sighed. "Clowns are often sad people. The makeup, costumes, jokes, and pratfalls are smoke and mirrors."

Charlotte slowed down slightly. The exhaust from the car stank.

"Have you any idea who the killer might be?"

"No, we're still in the throws of the investigation. Do you have any idea who it could be?"

Charlotte said nothing. She stared at the gravel as they walked on. DeKok did not press her. After a while she started talking again.

"Did you ever see any of his performances?"

DeKok made a regretful gesture.

"No, never."

She breathed deeply.

"That's really a pity. You should not have missed it. Pieter was one of a kind. Usually I waited in the wings for him, but one time I sat with the audience instead. It was almost magical. Pieter could keep any audience in a trance."

DeKok leaned his head forward and let the water run from the brim of his hat.

"Inimitable?"

"Absolutely. Holland will never have another Pierrot.

"You loved him?"

A tired smile played around her lips.

"Love, well, I don't know. Romantic love has always eluded me. Rather than a grand passion, it seems I have Fantinelli to nurture. He's a great, awkward, and helpless child. Perhaps that's why I'm always in pursuit of men."

"Like the clown?"

"Yes, like the clown ... like so many."

Again a silence fell between them. The rain increased, became more insistent. DeKok looked at the gravestones, reading the dates of birth and death. Most people, he realized with a start, did not live very long. He changed his gaze back to the hearse and thought about Charlotte's words.

"You really think he couldn't be replaced?"

"Who?"

"Pierrot."

Charlotte shook her head decisively.

"Impossible."

"But it happened. On the night that Pierrot's corpse was discovered, another Pierrot performed in Groningen. From what I hear, he performed flawlessly.

"Are you sincere?" There was disbelief in her voice.

DeKok nodded.

"Nobody, not on stage and not in the audience, noticed a difference."

Charlotte stopped. The hearse purred on. She wiped the water out of her eyes with the back of her hand. There was a dark look in her bright, green eyes.

"Butterfly ... she was the only person who knew Pierrot's act inside out."

16

Vledder looked at DeKok in amazement.

"Butterfly," he exclaimed, dazed. "It was Butterfly in Groningen?"

DeKok nodded complacently.

"According to Charlotte, Butterfly was capable of doing Pierrot's act, almost to perfection. She had done it for the group a few times, just as a joke."

"How would we ever prove that?"

DeKok nodded in agreement. His face was somber.

"The more I think about it, no two people could have mimicked him. We've only looked at Butterfly as a sweet, little dancer. By her own admission, she didn't have much of an impact alone. She hung at the end of a cable with some plastic wings. We saw her as a possible lead to the jewels. We completely ignored her musical background. Pierrot's act consisted largely of musical jokes, masterfully executed. Butterfly studied violin at the Conservatory. She probably played other instruments. Over the years, as a member of the group, she must have seen Pierrot's act hundreds of times. She must have absorbed every movement, every gesture."

Suddenly Vledder's eyes widened.

"But if ..." he said, stumbling over his words in haste, "if she, Butterfly, performed that night in Groningen ...

then ... then she must have *known* the murderer *and* his plans."

"That seems a reasonable assumption."

Vledder became more excited.

"He had plans—she acquiesced. She knew what was about to happen and agreed. That's why she traveled to Groningen while ..."

" ... Pierrot was being killed," completed DeKok.

"Yes."

Abruptly DeKok stood up, an exasperated look on his face.

"No, Dick. There's something wrong with our reasoning. I said it before; the victim did not need an alibi. The murderer needed an alibi. To turn it around is absurd." He pointed at Vledder. "What did Butterfly achieve with her performance in Groningen?"

"Eh, the impression ... she made us believe Pierrot was still alive."

"Very good. And what is the purpose of that, now that we know he's dead?"

Vledder swallowed when he saw the implication.

"To obscure the time of death."

"Right. What about the corpse?"

"Someone has to hide it, so it isn't found right away."

DeKok grinned evilly.

"And what does our murderer do? At almost the same time Butterfly appears onstage in Groningen as the living, breathing Pierrot ... the murderer dresses Pieter Eikelbos in his distinctive clown's costume. He places the body at the foot of Criers' Tower, in plain view. You see, and *that's* what I don't understand." DeKok paused for a moment and then continued in a milder tone of voice.

"What happened with that speedboat?"

Vledder had to gather his thoughts to adjust to the new twist the conversation had taken.

"The Water Police," he began, "at this time of the year, they're inundated. Sorry, no pun intended ... I mean they are swamped ... oops, never mind. There are a lot of reports about stolen boats of all types, mostly small boats. It seems to be a trend. Anyway, they had not yet searched for the owner of the speedboat. I took a good look at it and asked around Inner Side Canal. The boat almost certainly belonged to Pieter Eikelbos. According to the neighbors, a speedboat like that was usually moored alongside the deck outside his bedroom."

"So we know how they transported the corpse. It must be why the windows were opened from the inside, leaving no indication of forced entry."

The phone rang. Vledder picked it up and listened. After a few seconds he looked up at DeKok.

"Guess who's waiting for us downstairs?"

"Maurice Vlaanderen," answered DeKok without hesitation.

"How did you know?"

DeKok flashed a secretive smile.

"Weren't we going to send out an APB for his arrest?"

DeKok's expression did not change.

"Why go to all the trouble of searching for someone ... if they're going to report, anyway."

"No," screamed Maurice Vlaanderen. "You think I'm crazy? I didn't kill her. When I left, she was still alive."

"When was that?"

"Day before yesterday, the night before she was found murdered."

"What time?"

"About eleven o'clock. Yes, it was almost eleven o'clock when I left. Altogether I spent, maybe, an hour there."

"To do what?"

"To talk."

"What about?"

"Jewelry, what else?"

"Did she have the jewels?"

"She denied it."

DeKok leaned back in his chair and nodded at Maurice with an amiable smile on his face.

"Let's start at the beginning. How did you find out about Butterfly?"

Maurice closed his eyes while he thought.

"You know," he said slowly, "my father could only remember the word, or concept, *Butterfly* after the disappearance of his collection. Over Father's protest I told you about it." He lowered his head in shame. "By now you must know I was once arrested for the theft of some jewelry. When it comes to jewelry, I'm my father's son. I have the same fascination, the same love of stones. Even though my conviction dates back more than ten years, I did not want to be a suspect. So I was ready to do anything possible to resolve this matter for my father. On reflection I couldn't sit on the sidelines. I had to do something proactive."

"Acting as a private investigator."

Maurice smiled faintly.

"You could call it that. I went looking for Butterfly ... whoever or whatever that might be. Among others I asked a friend who's involved in theater, including the Municipal

Theater. He told me he had heard of a female dancer called Butterfly. She performed, primarily, in variety. I started calling impresarios."

"Peter Dongen among them."

"Yes," nodded Maurice. "Eventually I reached Peter Dongen. He gave me the phone number and address of the Butterfly he knew." He leaned in and said, in a confidential tone, "Look, inspector, my father remembered a Butterfly and suddenly it appeared there *was* a Butterfly. From the moment Dongen confirmed the dancer's stage name, I felt she had something to do with the robbery."

"Her actual name was Martha Hagen. Your father did not recognize her body."

Maurice Vlaanderen licked his dry lips.

"He told me. He told me over the phone. That's also the reason I immediately came here."

"You were in a hurry to get away?"

Maurice grimaced as he shook his head vehemently.

"No, it was not an attempt to flee. My absence from home overnight meant nothing. I was not about to disappear, and I beg you not to interpret my departure that way. I had no idea Butterfly, Martha Hagen, was dead. It was in the newspapers this morning."

"Do you still maintain Butterfly had something to do with the robbery at your father's house?"

"Pretty much—nothing has compelled me to change my mind," confessed Maurice.

DeKok looked stern.

"A bad assumption for a policeman."

Young Vlaanderen leaned back and gesticulated agitatedly with both hands.

"Look, I know I'm not a policeman. Honestly, I didn't

want to be. It was about wanting to recover my father's jewelry."

"You were willing to do anything to achieve that goal?"

"Yes."

"Even murder?"

Maurice jumped up.

"If you accuse me once more of murder," he roared, "I'll leave."

DeKok looked unimpressed.

"*If* I permit you to go."

Maurice calmed down suddenly and sat down again.

"Are you arresting me?"

"If you give me cause, yes," said DeKok.

Maurice Vlaanderen paled.

"You can't arrest me for her murder, when I'm not guilty."

DeKok shrugged nonchalantly.

"The Law gives me all sorts of options, besides suspicion of murder. I could hold you for domestic disturbance, threats of violence, or blackmail. Need I continue?"

"But I, I'm not guilty of any of those things."

DeKok grinned.

"You must admit anyone could be justified in suspecting you. We could book you on suspicion. You see, I'm sure Butterfly did not allow you in her apartment because she trusted your face. During your first telephone call you threatened her with prison if she did not return the jewels."

Maurice closed his eyes and sighed.

"There was nothing else to do. As we agree, I am not a police officer. He fell silent and raked his fingers through his hair. Then he changed his tone of voice. "You are correct.

I did put pressure on Martha Hagen. I forced a personal interview." There was pleading look in his eyes. "I could not afford to wait until all that gorgeous, antique jewelry had been melted down, perhaps moved across the border."

DeKok disregarded the remarks.

"So, she granted you the interview?"

"Yes."

"Under what kind of threat?"

Maurice lowered his head.

"I told her I would visit her with a few friends, and we'd destroy everything in the apartment."

"Not nice."

Young Vlaanderen shook his head.

"No, you're right. In retrospect I'm very sorry about it. Had she refused I would not have made good. I certainly have no friends who would engage in such a despicable act."

DeKok pulled out his lower lip and let it plop back. He repeated the offensive gesture several times. Maurice looked away.

"Eventually our little Butterfly capitulated."

Maurice turned back to face DeKok.

"Yes," he said. "She invited me to come and talk. We agreed on ten o'clock." He unbuttoned his top shirt button and ran a hand inside his collar. "It was to be all or nothing. She received me coolly. The conversation didn't go well. I told her about my father, his passion for jewelry. I told her he recalled only one word after the theft. It all meant nothing to her. She admitted to being called 'Butterfly,' but that was all. She knew nothing about any jewels and knew nothing about any theft."

"Then what?"

Maurice covered his eyes.

"She made me so angry. I went to her dressing table and drew out all the drawers." He took his hands away and stared into the distance. "All that time she remained seated on that hassock ... then she suddenly stood up and said, 'Your father will get the jewelry back.'"

DeKok's mouth fell open and for a moment he was speechless.

"What!?"

Maurice Vlaanderen nodded. He looked exhausted.

"She said she would bring the collection to him at noon, today."

17

DeKok needed a few moments to recover. He stood up and started to pace up and down the detective room. The revelations Maurice made were beyond his wildest imagination. This development was too much to absorb all at once. Ever since he had found her with a knife in her back, he had known Butterfly occupied a key position in the case. But he never dreamt she was *that* close.

His thoughts came to a standstill. He calmed himself, walked back to his desk, and resumed his seat. He leaned closer to Maurice.

"Did she explain?"

"Pardon me?"

DeKok gestured impatiently.

"How could she promise your father would get his jewelry back? How would she know exactly which jewels or which pieces of jewelry you were talking about?"

Maurice shook his head.

"I'm sorry to admit I didn't ask, maybe because of my conviction she was involved in the robbery. I never, quite frankly, doubted her complicity. When she said, 'Your father will get the jewelry,' I took it at face value. Afterward my relief resulted in a sudden impulse to leave town; I just wanted to celebrate the outcome with some friends. You can imagine how shocked I was when I heard of her death."

DeKok nodded his understanding.

"It was your strong belief she actually had the jewelry?"

"Definitely."

DeKok rubbed his chin.

"Why the extra day? Why not promise to return the jewels the next day, rather than the day after?"

Vlaanderen looked dumbfounded.

"I never gave it a thought. Her promise was enough for me. Later I reasoned she might need the extra time to retrieve the jewels from some secret location."

DeKok rubbed the back of his neck.

"You're not much help," he said sadly.

His visitor made a helpless gesture.

"I'm sorry, truly. Perhaps I'm too optimistic, or not bright enough, to get all the ramifications."

DeKok held the younger man with his eyes.

"Did it ever occur to you that Butterfly's promise might have meant nothing? Perhaps she was just trying to get rid of you and be done with your boorish behavior."

For a moment the broker's son looked deflated. But he quickly recovered. With a resolute gesture Vledder admired, he stretched out a finger to DeKok.

"The woman, Martha, Butterfly, *had* that jewelry."

Maurice Vlaanderen left DeKok and Vledder in the room with only the single sound of a humming defective light fixture. From the street came the tuneless voice of a drunk singing a tearjerker about betrayed friendship. It all passed by DeKok. He searched mentally for an explanation of the dimension Butterfly's demise added to both cases.

Vledder looked beat.

"Tell me what you think, DeKok," he said after some contemplation. "There's a common thread in these two murders."

"Between what?" asked DeKok, roughly torn from his own thoughts.

"The two murders. Here's a thought: Pierrot says he's going to pay off gambling debts with the jewelry, then someone kills him. Butterfly promises to return the jewelry to Vlaanderen, then someone kills her."

Vledder suddenly had all of DeKok's attention.

"That is indeed an aspect I find remarkable. I hadn't thought it through. You may have stumbled on the motives for the killings." He frowned, he liked the idea. "Both," he continued, "must have known the someone who had the jewels. Perhaps they'd known for some time. Simply knowing this secret didn't make either a real threat. The secret only became deadly once—" He stopped talking suddenly. The drunk outside had reached the second verse of his song: "What a friend ... what a friend you were to me." With a shock he came back to reality. He ran to get his coat and started to leave the room. Vledder laughed, despite himself. DeKok revved to top speed was comical indeed.

"What's the matter?" he asked, catching up with his older partner.

DeKok wrenched open the door. He talked as he ran down the stairs.

"The Garden. I need to see a friend on Daisy Street. Henri Jonkers was missing from Pieter Eikelbos' funeral."

Vledder lashed the few horses under the hood of the VW

hard. Traffic was passable at this time of night. They quickly crossed the dam and passed behind the Royal Palace. Before long they reached Roses Canal. It was the edge of the Jordaan.

DeKok slapped his forehead.

"Man I'm getting old! What a stupid mistake—was a time when I'd have gotten it right away. Why would Henri Jonkers stay away from the funeral of his boyhood acquaintance? It would be unthinkable for him to stay away of his own free will."

"What do you think happened to him?"

"Not the slightest idea."

Vledder risked a glance at his passenger.

"A knife in the back?"

DeKok did not answer. He braced himself with arms and legs as Vledder took a turn on two, screaming tires.

"You know where it is?"

"Yes," answered Vledder curtly. "Just behind Aster Street."

He forced the car around some obstacles, braking hard in the middle of Daisy Street.

Both inspectors vaulted out of the car at a dead run toward number 317. Vledder sprinted ahead, but DeKok, despite his odd gait, was not far behind. One after the other they took the narrow stairs two at a time. They were both out of air by the time they reached the third floor.

DeKok looked around and silently approached a door. He turned the knob and found the door locked. He signaled Vledder. The young inspector took a few steps backward and kicked hard. The hinges snapped and the door fell with a bang onto the kitchen floor.

The small living room was turned inside out. Furniture

was scattered around and all of the drawers and closets had been emptied on the floor.

They found Henri Jonkers in the small bedroom behind the living room. His hands and feet were tied to the bedposts with ropes. A piece of duct tape covered his mouth. His eyes expressed his gratitude and relief, as he recognized the inspectors.

DeKok quickly removed the duct tape, while Vledder cut the ropes with his pocketknife.

His face distorted with pain, Henri rubbed his chafed wrists and ankles. Suddenly he covered his eyes and burst into tears.

Vledder brought a glass of water from the kitchen. DeKok sat down on the edge of the bed.

Slowly Henri Jonkers regained his composure. He closed his eyes for a moment.

"Not knowing was the worst. To the end I didn't know whether someone would find me." He looked at DeKok. "How did you know?"

The gray sleuth shook his head regretfully.

"I'm sorry to say I didn't know. I missed you this morning at Pieter's funeral." He glanced at his watch. "I didn't put two and two together until about fifteen minutes ago."

Henri Jonkers sighed deeply. He drank some more water.

"It was last night, around ten o'clock. I was watching television. Without warning two men wearing ski masks broke in. They rushed me, dragged me to the bedroom, and tied me to the bed. Once my mouth was taped they ransacked my place."

"They were looking for jewels."

Jonkers looked surprised.

"Whatever it was they didn't find it," he stammered. "I don't have any jewels ... what kind of jewelry would a man like me have?"

"We're talking about a jewelry collection Pieter offered in payment of his gambling debts."

Henri Jonkers rubbed his mouth with the back of his hand. The traces of the duct tape were still visible.

"Pieter had this valuable collection?" he asked. "You're certain he offered them to someone?"

DeKok nodded.

"Yes. And I'm convinced that's the reason for your unwelcome guests. Freddie Wezel had to have known you and Pieter were close friends."

Henri made a helpless gesture.

"Of course he knew. Sometimes I accompanied Pieter when he went gambling. He even introduced me to Freddie." He thought for a while. "But Pieter had no jewels at all to offer anyone."

"You know that for a fact?"

"Absolutely."

DeKok shrugged.

"Then he must have thought he could lay his hands on enough jewelry to pay his debts."

Jonkers grinned without mirth.

"By what means, I would like to know?" His question was genuine.

DeKok looked sideways at Henri.

"Have you heard the troupe's dancer, Butterfly, was also murdered?"

"I read that."

"Did you know her?"

Henri Jonkers shook his head.

"No, much to my regret, I never met her in person. I only knew of her through Pieter."

"What did he tell you?"

Jonkers showed a melancholy smile.

"Ach, he shared small anecdotes from backstage. One time her plastic wings fell off—she had taken only a few steps. The stage manager refused to pull up on the cable, said she couldn't fly without wings. So there she stood. It must have been embarrassing and comical." He paused and took another sip of water. "I did get the impression Butterfly was well regarded by the company. Pieter always spoke about her with a certain tenderness."

DeKok sighed deeply.

"Nonetheless, she is dead. Just like Pieter, she had one of Fantinelli's throwing knives in her back."

Henri Jonkers stared at the wall.

"Unbelievable." There was a world of sorrow in his voice. "Incomprehensible. Where is the sense in it? It must be the work of some maniac."

DeKok did not react to the observation. He narrowed his eyes. Then he spoke, as if thinking out loud.

"You know what I don't understand? Butterfly was a soft, sweet, young woman. She had charm, natural beauty. Yet we've found nothing about any romantic affairs."

Henri Jonkers gave DeKok a surprised look.

"She had a long-term love affair," he said.

"An affair?" repeated DeKok.

Jonkers nodded emphatically.

"With a hypnotist."

"What?"

Jonkers nodded again.

"They lived together for years."

It was the second time within a few hours that DeKok's mouth fell open and he was speechless.

18

Vledder looked serious.

"Little Lowee," he said with determination, "will have to speak out. He'll have to talk."

"What about?"

Vledder waved his arms.

"About his acquaintance with whoever searched that houseboat. We could let it slip by—I know you'd rather keep it under the official radar. But not in light of what they did to poor Henri. Now it's gone beyond the pale. Who knows what would have happened had you not given him a second thought. He could have died a gruesome, slow death."

DeKok nodded but he had not heard a thing. His thoughts were otherwise occupied. He mulled over Henri Jonkers' story about Butterfly and her hypnotist lover. A door was, at least, ajar following the revelation. Suddenly there was a whole string of new perspectives. He contemplated his options for further opening of the door. What would he find, once he succeeded? The misery of being unable to connect it all remained. New perspectives, or not, he kept accumulating loose, unrelated, and extraneous facts. Where was the common thread? It had to be somewhere. He looked at Vledder.

"Find out whether Kuster is on duty. If so, ask him to come up for a moment."

Vledder lifted the telephone. DeKok placed both elbows on the desk and rested his chin on folded hands. His face became very pensive as he stared into the distance. He stopped noticing his surroundings. He wondered how he could have neglected to think about the hypnotist. In retrospect it seemed so obvious. DeKok knew the hypnotist would be the last individual he would consider. He was in denial about hypnosis and those who practiced it. Personally he could not imagine anyone would be able to partially suspend his will and influence his behavior. He would choose otherwise.

What is hypnosis? He understood it as an extreme form of suggestion. Hypnotists, so far as he knew, wielded a psychic influence, capable of transporting a subject to a state of mind in which all critical judgment is suspended. The subject follows all instructions and orders from the hypnotist without question. Had that happened to Vlaanderen and the other robbery victims in The Hauge? Had they opened their own safes, compelled by instructions received during hypnotic states? Would they have literally opened the way for thieves to take whatever they wanted? He recalled there hadn't been any need to fuss and bother with locks, codes, or what have you.

Vlaanderen had spoken of "blacking out of a gap in time." He remembered only a single word, "Butterfly." However, confronted with the corpse of Butterfly, Vlaanderen failed to recognize her.

Kuster entered the detective room. DeKok greeted him with a smile.

"Have a seat, Jan," he said in a friendly tone of voice. "I would like to talk some more about that party you organized for your soccer club."

"You found the money for another one?"

"No, but who knows? Perhaps I can persuade a grateful broker to make a donation in the near future."

"Let's hope so. It would be nice," said Kuster.

"Yes," DeKok said, "but right now I need your help. As I remember, at the time of your, eh, twenty-fifth anniversary, there was a hypnotist among the performers of that variety group."

"Yes."

"What did he do?"

Kuster grinned.

"He asked for volunteers from the audience. Then he made them perform all kinds of antics. When he said they were on a bicycle, they started to peddle. If he said they were on a horse, they started to move as if they were riding. It was comical, but for me, as a cop, it was also a bit uncomfortable. He even invited members of the management onto the stage. These were people I knew in my capacity as treasurer. I knew them to be solid, sober, and responsible people. But they were completely subjected to the will of the hypnotist during the sessions. That caused me to think. I remember discussing it with my wife, afterward. To everyone's astonishment none of the subjects recalled their silly behavior while on stage. They flat refused to believe it when told about it. I wondered whether it would be easy to make someone perform the most horrible crimes using hypnosis."

DeKok shook his head.

"Fortunately not. It seems people cannot be influenced to commit deeds under hypnosis that they aren't inclined to do naturally."

"Still, it was eerie."

DeKok nodded, his thoughts far ahead of the conversation.

"Would you recognize him?"

"Who?"

"The hypnotist."

Kuster grimaced.

"I don't know."

"You recognized the magician."

Kuster nodded, a vague look in his eyes.

"Maybe if we were suddenly face to face ..." He did not complete the sentence. "As you know, a performer has many means of disguising his true identity. Theater people have makeup and costumes; some can imitate mannerisms, even stance. If you told me the magician performed as the hypnotist, after intermission ... I would be unable to prove otherwise."

"Are you telling me members of that group performed in more than one capacity, played multiple roles?"

"No. I mean I don't know. It is just, with limited knowledge of theater, it seems to me people who perform together for a long time might fill in for each other. I think the public is subtly deceived. There surely must be occasions when one, or more, can't perform. In spite of illness or personal difficulties, you know, the show must go on."

"Which is an elaborate way of saying you could not be sure of identifying individual members of the troupe."

"Yes, that's about it." Kuster reflected for a moment. "Sorry I couldn't offer much help," he added. "But you remember, DeKok, what Shakespeare said?"

For a long time the old inspector stared over Kuster's head. His face was expressionless and there was a dull gleam in his eyes. Slowly the words of the watch commander penetrated his consciousness. Then he looked at Kuster.

"You're right, Jan," he said slowly. "The world is a stage. What is the quote? *All the world's a stage. And all the men and women, merely players. They have their exits and their entrances. And one man, in his time, plays many parts.* Shakespeare said it long ago, but it is so timely. Society does force us to play many parts—the fiery lover, the aggrieved husband, the helpless victim in a bloody drama. I have become gray on the force. It often seems to me little remains of our much touted individual liberty, as we struggle with the realities of our daily lives."

Kuster grinned self-consciously.

"You're in a pessimistic mood."

DeKok did not answer. He stood up to retrieve his hat and coat. Vledder got up to follow him. Kuster looked surprised, then shrugged his shoulders and went back downstairs.

"Where are we going?" asked Vledder.

"To Little Lowee's"

"We're going to nail the creeps who turned those homes upside down and gave Jonkers such a bad time? You're going to ask him about them?"

"Nope. I want to know if he knows a hypnotist who plays with butterflies."

DeKok stared out of the passenger's side window of the old VW. Before them, in the gray evening fog, they could just make out the silhouette of The Criers' Tower. Vledder was ill at ease. He felt nervous and restless. He might have felt less on edge had the visibility been better. The faint, blurred lines of objects made this a dangerous expedition. It also gave anyone fleeing a distinct advantage.

He was there to meet the man who ultimately agreed to play a chancy role in the proceedings. His stipulation was meeting at or near Criers' Tower. He wanted to be as close as possible to the place where the corpse of his friend had lain, regardless of whether it sounded sentimental or, even, maudlin. Henri Jonkers wouldn't consider a different venue for the unmasking of the killer. In the end DeKok had agreed, reluctantly.

To cover the alleys and canals in the neighborhood, he had called in additional detectives from Warmoes Street. Stoops, Rijpkema, Zeegers, and Keizer were strategically posted. They were not members of the homicide squad, because DeKok thought it more important for them to be familiar with the precinct. Each had a detailed description of the suspect, furnished by Vledder. Appie Keizer was posted at the most likely meeting place. With his round face, accentuated by a farmer's cap and a burgundy suit, he looked like anything but a police officer.

Because he was not sure how the killer would travel, DeKok had also alerted the Water Police; down the road, in either direction, he had posted teams of motorcycle cops. Nobody in a boat could escape the Water Police, and the motorcycle cops would not loose any fleeing vehicle. Still, like Vledder, he felt uneasy. There were too many uncertainties—busy Gelder Quay and the public, who would be more inclined to help the fleeing suspect than the police.

He looked at Vledder behind the steering wheel. The young inspector looked straight ahead, sulking a bit. He felt excluded because DeKok had refused to give him a full explanation. His old partner turned toward him. Vledder's obvious discomfort was another worry.

"I can't explain everything," said DeKok apologetically.

"When you are on your own, you will see. It isn't always possible, nor is it good mentoring."

"What if the murderer doesn't show?"

"He'll be here," said DeKok, more confident then he felt.

"You're sure?"

"Yes, if your theory is correct."

Vledder's mouth fell open.

"We're acting on my theory?"

"Yes, yours ... your theory"

The young inspector grinned. Once he replied he did not seem happy. His voice had a sad undertone.

"Which theory?" he asked mockingly. "Over the last few hours I've spouted more than my usual slew of theories, none of them—" He suddenly pointed out the window. "Look, it's Henri Jonkers ... in a white suit."

DeKok looked at his watch.

"He's a bit early. It's only five minutes to ten."

"That white suit your idea?"

"Henri Jonkers is consumed by hatred," observed DeKok simply.

"For the murderer?"

DeKok nodded slowly.

"At first he wanted to come in a white clown's costume, like the one Pierrot's corpse wore when we retrieved it. The white suit he's wearing is a compromise. I finally agreed because Henri should be clearly visible to the killer. The murderer doesn't know Pierrot's friend. They never met."

Vledder sighed.

"Is Henri a decoy because he would be such a big threat to the killer? Do you really think he will act?"

DeKok made a helpless gesture.

"I have to stay positive. In spite of my best efforts we haven't many options. This emergency measure may give us a shot. Regardless, we want all the evidence we can get concerning the murders." He suddenly became fully alert. He focused his attention across the water to the narrow side of Gelder Quay. He instinctively sensed danger. Without another word he exited the car. Keeping along the edge of the canal, he walked toward Prince Henry's Quay.

Blending with the parade of prostitutes across the canal, he had spotted a man. The man was old, bent-over, with a long beard. He limped along, a walking stick in his left hand. The impression of "labored movement" was too emphatic. To DeKok's practiced eye, it was a tad overdone, not believable.

Always cautious, DeKok knew he must avoid detection by the elderly object of his attention. He carefully, but urgently, increased his pace, hoping to warn Henri and Appie Keizer, who was his closest officer.

He rounded The Criers' Tower in a wide circle. Instantly he realized, to his horror, he was too late. The elderly cripple had neared the unsuspecting Henri Jonkers. He dropped his cane and raised his right arm. A knife gleamed in the half-light. With tremendous, explosive force the knife reached Henri's back.

A woman screamed.

The knife clattered to the ground.

The graybeard fled, running toward DeKok. DeKok spread both arms, attempting to stop the man. The man hit him, but the force of the impact was too great. DeKok fell on his back. His ridiculous little hat rolled into the gutter. Laboriously he climbed to his feet. He could hear the scream of a braking car behind him, followed by a heavy thud. When he looked around, he saw the gray-beard in the roadway.

Vledder came running. DeKok and Keizer followed. The man was on his stomach, his face turned to one side. A thin stream of blood ran out of his ear.

Vledder bent down. He looked up, shocked.

"Peter Dongen, the impresario."

DeKok nodded and turned around. He walked over to his hat and picked it up.

There was a tear in his eye.

19

Mrs. DeKok opened the door with a welcoming smile. On the stoop in front of her house stood Appie Keizer and Dick Vledder. She greeted the young men heartily.

"Are there more coming?" she asked.

Appie Keizer shook his head.

"The others are on duty. They were unexpectedly called to another precinct to help out temporarily, with a so-called suicide."

"So-called suicide?"

Appie Keizer grinned boyishly.

"The forensics indicate murder."

Mrs. DeKok brought her index finger to her lips.

"Don't say anything about it to my husband. He might just up and leave."

"No he won't," said Vledder. "This is being handled by headquarters. Besides I want several explanations on our *current,* just completed case. He just cannot leave until he has explained himself fully."

"Good for you," said Mrs. DeKok. Vledder was one of her favorites.

She preceded them to the cozy living room. The man of the house was comfortably ensconced in a deep, leather armchair. He had slippers on his feet and a small table with a bottle of cognac and several snifters close by.

He invited the two young inspectors to seat themselves on the sofa across from him. With obvious delight he poured three glasses of cognac. DeKok's enjoyment of cognac was elevated to a kind of meditation. He handed two of the glasses to his visitors. Mrs. DeKok returned from the kitchen with several platters of delicacies.

The Dutch almost never drink unless they can eat as well. The custom carries over to bars and airlines where peanuts and other snacks are served. Mrs. DeKok's finger food was of a much higher quality, however. It included two kinds of croquettes and the obligatory variety of wonderful cheeses. There were also Indonesian satays, lean pieces of meat delicately marinated, stuck on small bamboo skewers, and roasted. They looked like miniature shis-ke-babs. There were pork, beef, and chicken satays on a hot plate.

The men looked approvingly at the food, but Vledder could not contain his curiosity and impatience.

"Is he dead?"

DeKok rocked the snifter in his hand and took a first tasting sip. He did not answer until he had fully appreciated the golden liquid.

"He's hanging on. I was at the hospital this morning and the nurses permitted me to talk to him briefly. He seems very alert, mentally clear. But the attending physician still considers him critical."

"How did you know it was Peter Dongen?"

DeKok took another, bigger sip and then replaced his glass on the table.

"It was a long shot. The Vlaanderen jewelry collection touched the lives of so many in that variety troupe. That's why I was circumspect in approaching the subject with all the members. They seemed to be guarding some communal secret."

He selected a satay and ate it properly by holding the bamboo skewer horizontally in front of his mouth. He closed his teeth on a piece of meat and neatly pulled it off the skewer, moving the skewer away from his mouth in a sideways direction. He chewed with relish. The remaining two pieces of meat disappeared just as expeditiously. He placed the used skewer on an empty plate provided for the purpose.

Vledder watched him eat in silence.

"Come on, DeKok," he urged, "don't give it to us in installments."

"Sorry," said DeKok. "When Henri Jonkers told me about Butterfly's affair with a hypnotist, I felt it was the key to solving the mysterious thefts. Hypnosis. It occurred to me the victims might have opened their own safes while under hypnosis. Once each came out of his trance, he could recall only one word, *Butterfly*. It became critical to answer the question: Who was the hypnotist? Obviously we could have asked one of the group members. On reflection I felt I shouldn't, because of my earlier sense of a conspiracy of silence. The worst thing would have been to alert or alarm our suspect. I wanted, above all, to avoid having the suspect disappear altogether."

Under the disapproving eyes of Vledder, he interrupted his discourse to take another sip of cognac. But he soon enough started talking again.

"Even though Jan Kuster," he continued, "had seen the entire group perform at a party for his soccer club, he couldn't recall the hypnotist's name. However he did give me a usable description when I pressed him. He described a tall, wide-shouldered man with steel-blue eyes and a deep voice."

"Peter Dongen."

DeKok nodded.

The next hurdle was getting evidence. There was no solid proof. There was also the chance Dongen, apart from his involvement in the thefts, was involved in the murders. I even toyed with the thought of breaking into Dongen's place at Willem Park Way. We needed evidence. I was clutching at straws, you see. But my friend Henkie was on holiday, and I didn't think I would succeed on my own." DeKok looked at Keizer. "This goes no further than this room, eh?"

Keizer hastened to assure DeKok that he would keep his confidence.

"I understand," said Keizer, a grin on his face.

Vledder drained his glass and placed it on the coffee table in front of him.

"You said something, last night, about *my* theory?"

A smile fled across DeKok's face while he held the bottle up with a questioning gesture. Both men nodded their agreement. Mrs. DeKok had a sherry. Once the glasses were filled, DeKok picked up the thread of his narration.

"You observed a similarity in the timing of the deaths of Pierrot and Butterfly. Strangely, both were killed after they confessed to having the jewelry. It was a useful theory, one I decided to test." He sighed. "Also, I had come to the conclusion that there was only one way to catch the killer … I had to entice him into attempting a third murder."

"How?" asked Keizer.

"*How* indeed. I decided to discuss the matter with Henri Jonkers. After some persuading, he agreed to cooperate.

He wrote a letter to Dongen. He wrote to say, as Pierrot's only remaining friend, he was fully aware of the jewelry. He went on to say he had proof Peter Dongen had murdered his friend. He gave a few more details and demanded his, that is Pieter's, share of the loot."

"Hey," interrupted Keizer, "what's with Peter, Pieter, and Pierrot ... just *how* many people are you talking about?"

"Two," explained Vledder briefly. "Pierrot is the stage name of Pieter Eikelbos, the clown. Peter Dongen is an impresario and, as we now know, a murderer."

"Yes," said DeKok. "Henri also added a blackmail clause to his letter. He threatened to involve the police if he did not get his share of the loot."

Keizer snorted in admiration.

"A diabolical plot."

DeKok readily agreed.

"It wasn't just diabolical, it was downright dangerous. You see, Henri Jonkers insisted the meeting between him and Dongen take place near Criers' Tower. It was dangerous for him and difficult for us. We could not just throw out a dragnet, for fear Dongen would smell a rat and disappear. The trap had to be left open, meaning we could not fully protect Henri. Since I figured that the killer would use a knife, Henri wore a thin, steel plate, front and back, beneath his coat."

"That's why the knife did not penetrate."

They took time to eat something. DeKok was pensive as he drained his glass. On his own accord he resumed.

"I hadn't figured on Dongen disguising himself as an old man. Although everyone had a fairly accurate description, he was unrecognizable. Pure luck and a child's exercise helped me spot him among all those working girls across the canal. He was the element out of place in the picture. His running smack into a passing car is something I could not have foreseen ... or wished."

There was another long silence. Everybody nibbled something and DeKok refilled the glasses once again. Mrs. DeKok left for the kitchen to make coffee. Vledder eventually broke the companionable silence.

"But I still don't understand the how and why of those murders."

DeKok was ready to answer.

"A policeman," he began slowly, "sometimes comes to hasty conclusions. We found the clown with the knife in his back. Later we discovered the knife belonged to Fantinelli. It smacked of a planned, premeditated, murder. It seemed to me the killer had stolen the knives to commit murder with them."

"And that wasn't so?" asked Vledder, surprised.

"No, the case with knives was stolen by a drug addict. The junkie took them to a fence and got a pittance. The fence took a good look at the case and discovered Fantinelli's name on the inside of the lid. He quickly realized the knives would be worth a lot more to the knife thrower than to anyone else. He tried to contact Fantinelli. That's how he reached the impresario, Dongen, who immediately bought back the knives."

"In order to use them in a murder," opined Keizer.

"No, that's the tragic part. Dongen was not a killer ... not at first. He just wanted the best for everybody. That's why I hope he makes it."

"You cannot be serious. He committed two murders!"

"Yes, Dick. Think about what happened? This was his

group, one in which he participated as a hypnotist. It went broke and quickly went under because of Pierrot's gambling. The debts mounted, engagements dried up, and people were beginning to disband. Over the years, these people supported each other, personally and professionally. They were a family. A number of them wanted to keep the cohesiveness of the group ... wait for better times. For their survival, Peter Dongen offered to use his hypnotic gifts for criminal activities. To hide his nefarious activities, he settled in as impresario at Willem Park Way. The others agreed with the plan and promised to cooperate, whenever necessary."

"That's how a variety troupe turned into a criminal gang," said Keizer, smirking.

"You could say that," smiled DeKok. "Peter Dongen, who knew something about jewelry, started to visit auctions, charity events, and estate sales. When he identified a likely prospect, he would hypnotize the person. The rest was simplicity itself. He persuaded the individual to open his own safe to show off his jewelry collection. All the victims opened their safes under hypnosis. Peter Dongen then appropriated the jewelry, cash, and other valuables."

"Cash and other valuables?" asked Vledder.

"Yes."

"I thought only jewelry was stolen. I did not see anything about cash and other valuables ... what valuables?"

DeKok grinned.

"There are quite a number of people in our beloved country who keep undeclared cash, stocks, and bonds in their safe. The tax man knows nothing about it."

"Aha, assets kept under the table?"

"Precisely. The stolen jewelry, which is almost always insured, is reported. But the money, on which no tax has been paid, is another matter. It's cheaper to write off the loss than risk getting a late assessment from Inland Revenue."

"What did Dongen do with the cash?"

"He maintained the group. Every one received a generous share."

"And the jewelry?"

"He kept it in his safe at Willem Park Way. The group voted not to liquefy it, yet. They were just waiting for Dongen to stop his activities. They felt it would be safer once the press and rumors about the thefts subsided."

Vledder was upset.

"So they *all* knew about the jewels!?"

"Certainly, but it was in their collective interests to keep silent."

"I'm starting to understand ... the trouble started when Pierrot offered the jewelry as payment for his gambling debts."

DeKok sighed.

"Yes, Pierrot was at his wit's end when he offered the jewelry to Freddie Wezel. He tried to convince Dongen to release a portion of the loot, but Dongen refused. He discussed it with Butterfly and they decided Pierrot had to disappear for a while. Dongen has a summer cottage in the country, a perfect hiding place. To avoid complications and mislead Freddie, they decided Butterfly would take over Pierrot's act. Friday night before the performance in Groningen, Dongen stole Pierrot's costume from his car. On Monday, Butterfly took off for Groningen."

"And what about Dongen?"

"Dongen went to Pierrot's houseboat. He had the knives with him. He intended to give them to Charlotte, so she could return them to Fantinelli. Then he was to take

Pierrot to the cottage. But Pierrot wouldn't hear of it. He refused to disappear, did not want to go to the cottage. He promised a scandal should Butterfly *dare* to perform in his place. Worse, he threatened to go the police, unless Dongen immediately turned over the jewels so he could pay his gambling debts."

Mrs. DeKok entered with a tray, laden with a coffeepot and the usual accompaniments. Vledder and Keizer both jumped up to help her.

"Just make some room on the coffee table," she said. "Then you can help yourselves."

After they were again settled, DeKok resumed.

"During the argument, Pierrot tried on the new costume Charlotte had made for him. Dongen felt betrayed. He had done everything to preserve the group, committed crimes. Now this clown, who was responsible for their troubles, was making demands. Something snapped. In a sudden rage, he grabbed a knife out of the case and pushed it into Pierrot's back."

DeKok closed his eyes for a moment. In his mind he reviewed the interview with the impresario.

"Pierrot," he said, "bled to death while Dongen watched, horrified. Rage had driven him to this desperate act. He decided to put the corpse on Freddie Wezel's doorstep. He was attempting to throw us off the scent. As soon as it got dark, he hoisted the corpse into Pierrot's speedboat and steered it to Gelder Quay. But what could he do—he found the canal walls were too high. There was no place in the immediate surroundings to unload the corpse."

"So he placed Pierrot on the little dock at the foot of Criers' Tower," said Vledder, once again exercising his tendency to say the obvious.

DeKok paused. He remembered his impressions as the case started. He could still see busy Gelder Quay, the bars of the fence, the knife in the back of the clown. But Vledder wanted to know more.

"Did he really place Butterfly in a praying attitude?" he asked.

"Yes, he confessed it. When Butterfly demanded the Vlaanderen jewelry, he found himself betrayed once again. Nevertheless he promised to deliver the jewels to her."

"And killed her."

DeKok poured a cup of coffee. Suddenly he had lost his appetite for cognac.

"Butterfly was the only one of the group with much religious background. She would attend church services occasionally. After he stabbed her, Peter placed her in the position we found. 'Pray,' he screamed, 'pray for *my* sins.' Then he left her."

"A strange man," commented Mrs. DeKok.

DeKok looked at his wife.

"Strange?" he questioned. "How does one judge a person *strange?* In my estimation, Peter Dongen is an intelligent, talented man. Granted he is temperamental; a man with an innate sense of the theater and the dramatic. He possesses a unique soul and a mind in which good and evil are too closely related. He lost his ability to separate one from the other."

They remained silent for a long time. By now everybody had switched to coffee. Slowly the impressions of the impresario and his crimes were replaced by other thoughts. The conversation became more general. It was already late when the two young inspectors left.

After they left, Mrs. DeKok pushed a hassock closer to her husband's chair.

"All night I have been waiting to hear just one thing," she said.

"And what is that?"

"Did Butterfly take part in the robberies?"

DeKok shook his head.

"Never."

"Then how was it possible for all those people to remember a Butterfly?"

DeKok reached over and retrieved his jacket from a nearby chair. He felt in one of the pockets and produced a pendant. It was an exquisite onyx, in the shape of a butterfly, set in a gold casing, studded with about two-dozen small, sparkling diamonds.

"A present from Butterfly to Peter Dongen while they were still in love. Peter used it in his act to hypnotize his subjects. Later he used it to hypnotize his victims."

The gray sleuth held the sparkling butterfly by the chain and slowly rocked it in front of his wife's eyes.

Mrs. DeKok looked at it, fascinated. Suddenly she looked into his eyes.

"Jurriaan … Jurriaan DeKok. You don't have to try and hypnotize *me*. You already did that … years ago, when we first met."

ABOUT THE AUTHOR

A. C. Baantjer is the most widely read author in the Netherlands. A former detective inspector of the Amsterdam police, his fictional characters reflect the depth and personality of individuals encountered during his near forty-year-career in law enforcement.

Baantjer was honored with the first-ever Master Prize of the Society of Dutch-language Crime Writers. He was also recently knighted by the Dutch monarchy for his lifetime achievements.

The sixty crime novels featuring Inspector Detective DeKok written by Baantjer have achieved a large following among readers in the Netherlands. A television series, based on these novels, reaches an even wider Dutch audience. Launched nearly a decade ago, the 100th episode of "Baantjer" series recently aired on Dutch channel RTL4.

In large part due to the popularity of the televised "Baantjer" series, sales of Baantjer's novels have increased significantly over the past several years. In 2001, the five millionth copy of his books was sold—a number never before reached by a Dutch author.

Known as the "Dutch Conan Doyle," Baantjer's following continues to grow and conquer new territory. According to the Netherlands Library Information Service, a single copy of a Baanjter title is checked out of a library more than 700,000 times a year.

The DeKok series has been published in China, Russia, Korea, and throughout Europe. Speck Press is pleased to bring you clear and invigorating translations to the English language.

Inspector DeKok Investigates
by Baantjer

DeKok and the Geese of Death

Renowned Amsterdam mystery author Baantjer brings to life Inspector
DeKok in another stirring potboiler full of suspenseful twists and
unusual conclusions.

ISBN: 0-9725776-6-1, ISBN13: 978-0-9725776-6-3

DeKok and Murder by Melody

"Death is entitled to our respect," says Inspector DeKok who finds
himself once again amidst dark dealings. A triple murder in the
Amsterdam Concert Gebouw has him unveiling the truth behind two
dead ex-junkies and their housekeeper.

ISBN: 0-9725776-9-6, ISBN13: 978-0-9725776-9-4

DeKok and Murder by Installment

Although at first it seemed to be a case for the narcotics division, it
soon evolves into a series of sinister and almost impossible murders.
Never before have DeKok and Vledder been so involved in a case
whereby murder, drug smuggling, and child prostitution are almost
daily occurences.

ISBN: 1-933108-07-X, ISBN13: 978-1-933108-07-0

Praise for the Inspector DeKok Series

"Along with such peers as Ed McBain and Georges Simenon, [Baantjer] has created a long-running and uniformly engaging police series. They are smart, suspenseful, and better-crafted than most in the field."
—*Mystery Scene*

"… an excellent and entertaining mystery from a skillful writer and profound thinker."
—*Midwest Book Review*

"Baantjer's laconic, rapid-fire storytelling has spun out a surprisingly complex web of mysteries."
—*Kirkus Reviews*

"This series is the answer to an insomniac's worst fears."
—*The Boston Globe*

"DeKok's maverick personality certainly makes him a compassionate judge of other outsiders and an astute analyst of antisocial behavior."
—*The New York Times Book Review*

"It's easy to understand the appeal of Amsterdam police detective DeKok; he hides his intelligence behind a phlegmatic demeanor, like an old dog that lazes by the fireplace and only shows his teeth when the house is threatened."
—*The Los Angeles Times*

"Shrewd, compassionate and dedicated, DeKok makes a formidable opponent for criminals and a worthwhile competitor for the attention of Simenon's Maigret fans."
—*Library Journal*

Boost

by Steve Brewer

Sam Hill steals cars. Not just any cars, but collectible cars, rare works of automotive artistry. Sam's a specialist, and he's made a good life for himself.

But things change after he steals a primo 1965 Thunderbird. In the trunk, Sam finds a corpse, a police informant with a bullet hole between his eyes. Somebody set Sam up. Played a trick on him. And Sam, a prankster himself, can't let it go. He must get his revenge with an even bigger practical joke, one that soon has gangsters gunning for him and police on his tail.

"… entertaining, amusing … . This tightly plotted crime novel packs in a lot of action as it briskly moves along."
—*Chicago Tribune*

"Brewer earns four stars for a clever plot, totally engaging characters, and a pay-back ending … ."
—*Mystery Scene*

ISBN: 1-933108-02-9 | ISBN13: 978-1-933108-02-5

Killing Neptune's Daughter

by Randall Peffer

Returning to his hometown was something Billy Bagwell always dreaded. But he felt he owed it to Tina, the object of his childhood sexual obsession, to see her off properly. Even in death she could seduce him to her. Upon his return to Wood's Hole on Cape Cod, Billy's past with his old friends—especially his best friend, present day Catholic priest Zal—floods his mind with classic machismo and rite-of-passage boyhood events. But some of their moments were a bit darker, and all seemed to revolve around or involve Tina … moments that Billy didn't want to remember.

This psycho-thriller carries Billy deeper and deeper into long-repressed memories of thirty-five-year-old crimes. As the days grow darker, Billy finds himself caught in a turbulent tide of past homo-erotic encounters, lost innocence, rage, religion, and lust.

"… the perfect book for those who fancy the darker, grittier side of mystery. A hit-you-in-the-guts psychothriller, this is a compelling story of one man's search for truth and inner peace."
—*Mystery Scene*

ISBN: 0-9725776-5-3 | ISBN13: 978-1-933108-05-6

Nick Madrid Mysteries
by Peter Guttridge

No Laughing Matter

Tom Sharpe meets Raymond Chandler in this humorous and brilliant debut. Meet Nick Madrid and the "Bitch of the Broadsheets," Bridget Frost, as they trail a killer from Montreal to Edinburgh to the ghastly lights of Hollywood.

ISBN: 0-9725776-4-5, ISBN13: 978-0-9725776-4-9

A Ghost of a Chance

New Age meets the Old Religion as Nick is bothered and bewildered by pagans, satanists, and metaphysicians. Seances, sabbats, a horse-ride from hell, and a kick-boxing zebra all come Nick's way as he tracks a treasure once in the possession of Aleister Crowley.

ISBN: 0-9725776-8-8, ISBN13: 978-0-9725776-8-7

Two to Tango

On a trip down the Amazon, journalist Nick Madrid survives kidnapping, piranhas, and urine-loving fish that lodge where a man least wants one lodged. After those heroics, Nick joins up with a Rock Against Drugs tour where he finds himself tracking down the would-be killer of the tour's pain-in-the-posterior headliner.

ISBN: 1-933108-00-2, ISBN13: 978-1-933108-00-1

The Once and Future Con

Avalon theme parks and medieval Excaliburger banquets are the last things journalist Nick Madrid expects to find when he arrives at what is supposedly the grave of the legendary King Arthur. As Nick starts to dig around for an understanding, it isn't Arthurian relics, but murder victims that he uncovers.

ISBN: 1-933108-06-1, ISBN13: 978-1-933108-06-3

Peter Guttridge is the Royal Literary Fund Writing Fellow at Southampton University and teaches creative writing. Between 1998 and 2002 he was the director of the Brighton Literature Festival. As a freelance journalist he has written about literature, film, and comedy for a range of British newspapers and magazines. Since 1998 he has been the mystery reviewer for *The Observer*, one of Britain's most prestigious Sunday newspapers. He also writes about—and doggedly practices—astanga vinyasa yoga.

Praise for the Nick Madrid Mysteries

"Highly recommended."
—*Library Journal*, starred review

"… I couldn't put it down. This is classic Guttridge, with all the humor I've come to expect from the series. Nick is a treasure, and Bridget a good foil to his good nature."
—*Deadly Pleasures*

"Guttridge's series is among the funniest and sharpest in the genre, with a level of intelligence often lacking in better-known fare."
—*Balitmore Sun*

"… one of the most engaging novels of 2005. Highly entertaining … this is humor wonderfully combined with mystery."
—*Foreword*

" … Peter Guttridge is off to a rousing start … a serious contender in the mystery genre."
—*Chicago Tribune*

"[The] Nick Madrid mysteries are nothing if not addictively, insanely entertaining … but what's really important is the mix of good suspense, fast-and-furious one-liners and impeccable slapstick."
—*Ruminator*

"… both funny and clever. This is one of the funniest mysteries to come along in quite a while."
—*Mystery Scene*

For a complete catalog of our books please contact us at:

speck press
po box 102004
denver, co 80250, usa
e: books@speckpress.com
t & f: 800-996-9783
w: speckpress.com

Our books are available through your local bookseller.